ALMOST DON'T COUNT

ALMOST DON'T COUNT

TALES OF AN AMERICAN FAILURE

F. CLAUDE DEROY

authorHOUSE®

AuthorHouse™
1663 Liberty Drive
Bloomington, IN 47403
www.authorhouse.com
Phone: 1 (800) 839-8640

Published by AuthorHouse 09/04/2015

ISBN: 978-1-5049-4891-3 (sc)
ISBN: 978-1-5049-4890-6 (e)

Chapter 1

Family

"Fuck you! You're an idiot! You're wasting your time pissing up a rope with that shit! If you spent half the time reading your school books like you do those joke books you might do something with your life!"

This was my father's response when I told him I was going to try performing stand-up comedy. My father was a high school dropout and saying this to his only son - with a 3.4 GPA in his senior year of high school.

"Nice," I thought. "Thanks for the vote of confidence!"

He never supported my dreams. My dreams were big, but not unreachable. Thirty years later I understood why. But this was then and how things went.

Hello there. My name is Roy and this is my story. Allow me to apologize if this gets a little hard to follow or confusing at times but, it's the way I talk. I'll simply write what happens the way it comes out as if I were telling it to you. Thank you in advance for understanding. I hope you can keep up. Here we go!

My dad, Roy Sr., was a large man, and his hands were huge- particularly when I felt them on my backside, although it wasn't that often. My mother on the other hand, was different. WAY different. My dad was to be my hero, what I got in the heaven's lotto of father's was a standoffish man that couldn't see life through any alternative perspectives. If it didn't make sense to him, it wasn't worth talking about. He was a bit self-centered, and a bit bitter and angry. It seemed he could never feel real joy for himself. But wow! He was funny. He was funniest guy in the world. He hid his pain, negativities, and doubts behind his sense of humor. I always hoped that I would inherit that ability. It seemed like the fun way to survive being miserable. One might as well find something to smile about.

How my folks wound up together is a book all on its own, but they did. They went to the same high school. I guess my mother was dared to go on a date with my dad. For whatever reason, she did. She even wound up having sex with him. This was 1964; they were teens, so no precautions were taken. So yes she got pregnant and used this as a ticket out of her bad situation at home.

They married young. My father was only eighteen. My mother was just sixteen. They got married for all the wrong reasons.

My mom, she was the eleventh child from her parents. My grandparents were breeders. They believed their purpose was to have as many kids as they could, but they stopped at eleven. My grandmother's body took a beating from birthing so many. Another one would have killed her.

Being the baby sibling in a large Italian family has its perks. If the child is a girl, it's even better. She is a princess. My mom was just that, a little Italian princess. She was spoiled pretty badly. She never had to do anything growing up. Everybody did things for her. She had no chores like doing the dishes, setting the table for dinner, or mopping, no dusting or even cleaning her room.

Things changed drastically after her 12th birthday though. My Grandmother became ill and passed away. Mom told the story of the night she died a couple times to me and my sisters. It's one of the saddest things I've ever heard. My grandmother was out walking in the rain and bad weather for a reason I must omit from this story. She was gone for three days and returned exhausted and with pneumonia. My mother waited intently for her each day while she was gone. One of those days was my mother's birthday. When my grandmother didn't even come home for her birthday my mother began to emotionally sink. She was scared for the worst.

But she did return. She came home about 8:45 in the evening after that third day. My grandmother walked in, lay back on the sofa, and closed her eyes. My mom was so excited when she heard her mom was there. She ran downstairs as fast as she could and lay down beside her. She wrapped her arms around her and said, "Mom I'm so glad you're home! I missed you so much." My grandmother took her last breath. She exhaled. She passed away right there.

My grandfather got over it pretty quick. It didn't take him to long before he was re-married to a second wife. And then had ten more children with her! Man, I couldn't imagine having a wife and eleven kids, then having to start over, let alone having ten more freaking kids the next round!! That's just insane. But wait, there's more… while he was creating his first family. He was not so faithful to his wedding vows. He was having extra marital affairs. He had a lot of them too. This was back in the day in the mid 1920's through the 1940's and condoms weren't so popular so he wound up producing some children through these affairs. Seven to be exact! He fathered seven more children with five more different women! Two of the women had two kids each; the other three got just one. The actual count was twenty-eight children. At that point you'd think to stop but he didn't. During his wave of creating offspring with the second wife, he was not faithful to her either. He impregnated six more women, giving him a grand total of thirty-four children. One man, thirteen women, thirty-four kids... he was dead at fifty-three years old.

Getting back to where I was... my mother's drastic change in life. After the emotional set back of dealing with losing her mother, life as she knew it changed. It happened the day my grandfather married the second wife. My mother, who was for so long the baby, was now the hated stepdaughter to the evil stepmother. She wasn't being protected by her "first family" status any longer. She was beaten, forced to play servant to her new mother, and new siblings. She had to cook and clean now. Her days of being the pampered baby of the family were over. My Grandfather was quite wealthy, so I can imagine how it felt for my mother going from one end of this spectrum to the other.

She wanted out, and jumped on the first opportunity that came across her path - my father.

My dad came from a large family too but his was the complete opposite. There were only nine children in his household. They weren't as fortunate with finances as my maternal grandparents were. My dad's father, Ray, my grandfather, was an alcoholic, very abusive, and the world's worst gambler.

One family story is that Ray once threw his wife (my grandmother) down a flight of steps and broke her leg when she was five months pregnant. And later, on the day when she had the baby, it was announced excitedly in the house that it was a girl. My father who was just a lad jumped up for joy and said, "Hooray! I have a baby sister!" My grandfather hit him in the head with a cast iron frying pan, cracking his skull. A short time after that, my grandfather placed a bet on a "sure thing" and lost their house in the deal.

My mom took on beatings and discipline but didn't have it as rough as my dad. She was a petite woman. I failed to mention previously that my mother is a natural Italian blonde. It's a rare occurrence that pops up in a generation from time to time. She was teased some in her early years by siblings. She hated having it. She would hide it in hats and wigs. In the 60s and 70s, loads of women wore wigs, bouffants, and scarves in their hair. It was no big deal, but for mom, it was a shameful thing. She longed for the dark hair and eyes of her sisters. She was the baby of the first brood and got lost in the shuffle through the second. She did stand out because of her hair and I think it messed her up a little the self-esteem department. She had very little. I believe that this fact here is the reason she took liking to my dad. He was funny and she had no confidence.

This was the beginning of my family and one bad decision after another. My parents eloped. It's funny to me, I think about it sometimes. It's funny because nobody does that anymore. Who elopes? Does anyone even know what it is? But my parents did. And by the time my mother was twenty-two, she was married for six years and about to give birth to her fifth child.

Chapter 2

Enter: Me

Being born is not an option. Nature does its thing. When a male and female do nature's thing, a real person is born. A person that will have their own individual perceptions, likes, dislikes wants, needs, desires, and dreams.

And there I was. No choice. No say in the matter. I was just there with my family. I had no idea how I got there. But, there I was. Like everyone else. Looking around, growing, and learning of things that were exposed to me.

At three or four years old I picked up on the fact that we lived different from other families. We didn't have what they had. Well technically we did have what they had. Most of everything we owned was a "hand me down", furniture, clothes and even cars.

At parties and barbeques we were looked at differently. Hearing the other adults pointing out things was confusing to me. To see them hug and kiss my parents when we got to the event and then say bad things about them behind their back didn't make sense. I remember being teased by a cousin for wearing a pair of yellow and lime green plaid bell bottoms jeans that were once his. This started the major complex I have. I wanted to retort but knew I had no legs to stand on. He had the best of everything. I was standing there wearing his old clothes and sporting the best shoes that "Goodwill" had to offer. The shoes were awful. I had to pull bird feathers out of them so I could put them on the first time. I think they were sitting in a chicken coop or something. They were blue but had white spots on them. My mom said it was just paint but I was no dummy. I still complained, "But mom! Those are bird feathers stuck in them!"

I knew we were poor. I never got anything new. We were so poor that I woke up three times on Christmas morning to no real presents. How can a kid call socks and underwear a gift? Or soap on a rope with a face cloth? What can a kid say? My best bet was to just keep my mouth shut and take the pain. My father quoted a scripture one time that stuck with me. It got me through times like this. "I felt bad because I had no shoes, then I met a man who had no feet." In other words, things could be worse. I did at least, have shoes. Then only thing I could do was just take the pain.

My sisters and I were the kids you saw with the woman in the check-out line holding up candy bars and packs of gum asking "mommy can I have this?" and always got a "no." She didn't have the money. She never had the money. Me, being of sound mind and body, learned that if I put in my pocket without anyone seeing it, I could keep it! I knew it was wrong. But I did it and got away with it. Apparently I was a little thief. I did it almost every time my mom took me into a store with her. I kept doing it and of course, I got caught. The first time I was caught stealing was at a local "mom and pop" convenience store down the street from our house. It was 1971; we were living in the outer rim of an inner city in the north east. I was probably four or five and walked down the block alone to the store. I don't remember what I was stealing or how I was caught but the store owner called my folks and had them pick me up. "You need money for everything you want." were the only words the clerk said to me. They echo in my head to this day from that experience.

So I started dreaming. I started dreaming of being wealthy. It's the dream I've had ever since. I realized I was poor and nobody. It's a dream that millions of kids have while growing up. Shortly after my first account with being caught stealing, my father had packed us up from the city, where we were all born, and moved us to the Midwest. I was about six years old. We moved from a house in the city to a trailer in a field. It was an adjustment I don't believe that can be made sanely. It's not the same kind of hot like in the city. There are things in the air like ragweed pollen and pollens from trees that we knew nothing about. But this is where my dreams began. I used to lie in bed at night and see spotlights in the sky going back and forth from the local car sales business thinking it was Hollywood. I'd see those lights scrape across the dark canvas of night and I would hear the intro music from a 20th Century Feature Film in my head. I wanted to live the lavish life of a movie star. All the money that comes with it could bring me happiness. I wished to be able to buy everything we needed. And of course I would think of how great it would be to have everyone taking my picture and asking me for an autograph. I longed for the better things. I knew the difference between name brand and knock off brands. But I wanted more than that. I wanted the royal life! I didn't want mom and dad to have to work anymore. I wished for my sisters & me to have better clothes, and for us to have a big house, so big we had to have maids and people we paid to take care of us. I loved my family. The true dream was to help my family live life, not just stay alive.

Although I wanted to be a star, I had no idea of how to be one or how to get there or what I would do if I did. I never strived for the goal and then this happened…

I was in first grade and I was given the lead role in a school play. It was a production of Uncle Remus' "Brear Rabbit and the Tar Baby" The excitement of all that went into putting on that show placed a bug in me forever. The stage prep and scene making and props and painting and practicing our lines were awesome. I loved everything involved with production. And the night of the play went off without a hitch. I remember one of my aunts had been the one to drop me off at the school because my parents could not bring me. Both of them told me they will be there before the play started.

I found myself looking for them in the crowd as the play finished. I wanted to wave at them from the stage like everyone else. That didn't happen. I couldn't find them. They weren't there. So I focused on the applause. It made me feel like I mattered. That play exploded my mind for the craft. Fame and fortune is what I wanted. I wanted to be rich beyond my wildest dreams.

The reality check came when I had to wipe the sweat from my brow and take focus on the room in which I rested. It was a room, in a trailer, where a wall on hinges opened up kind of like a door and separated the living room from a Murphy bed that was tucked up behind it. We had no air conditioning or ceiling fans to help with the midsummer Midwest mugginess. I shared this room with my two younger sisters, Ann and Marie.

Getting dressed and ready for school was always an ordeal. Three kids, a five, six, and a seven year old, in a five foot by seven foot Porto-room trying to put clothes on while stuffing a fold out bed up in a wall without killing each other is a nightmare every morning! All I could do was dream of how I wanted out of this situation, how I wanted my family to be in a better place.

My two older sisters, Mary and Linda had to share another room that had an actual door. It wasn't much bigger than the space the three of us younger kids got. My folks got the master bedroom which I think was a whopping ten foot by ten foot. Of course the trailer had the world famous wood stained paneling décor with the orange and brown shag carpet. The whole trailer wasn't more than thirty feet long and a mere ten feet wide. You can imagine how cramped it was. We didn't even have a living room. Well it did have a living room but we had to use it for the dining room. We kept the sofa and coffee table outside on a concrete pad next to the trailer and set a tarp up over it. The best thing about this place is it sat on a huge lot of land. It was a bit more than an acre. It was huge to me. The trailer sat off to the side in the back at the end of a dirt driveway. The rest was just a big front yard with no trees. Cutting the grass was a big ordeal because it grew tall like wheat! And of course it's not like we had a landscaping crew or even something to ride to cut it. It was a three day event to cut that stuff. I had this little raggedy clunker push mower that shut off every ten feet. I spend most of the time pulling the damn start cord.

After cutting the grass the first time, my dad had a big camping tent he set up. I recall it being fit to sleep thirteen people. It was set up for the whole summer. We slept in it every night and stayed out of the sun in it during the day. One day while we were playing inside of it my father came home with a brand new pool for us! It was three foot tall and eighteen feet across. That was a good moment in my life. I'm sure we would have survived without the pool but it helped us cope with the scorching summer temps. If it was all he could do for us, my dad did it.

It's obvious that gesture had lasting effects. I still think about those days. I can smile about some things. This is one of them.

I suppose my parents were doing the best they could with what they had to go on. The only thing they both ever knew was "the mom must always be pregnant". Fortunately, they stopped at five kids. I heard my mother say time and time again that all she wanted was boys. After four girls and only one boy they figured the odds and stopped. I'm the only boy and I'm right in the middle. All I have are sisters, two older and two younger, and we are all about one year apart. As a matter fact when I was eleven months old, my mother gave birth to my first younger sister Ann. I'm not even one year older than her. And we always had to celebrate our birthdays together. And there was always one cake decorated half boy stuff half girl stuff. I guess I feel like my thunder was taken. It's a classic case of "Middle Child Syndrome."

I think the "middle child syndrome" has a lot to do with my desire to be in the limelight. I always wanted to be the center of attention.

I didn't pine for it with my family as much as I did with friends. I believe that comes from watching my father have such good times with his friends. They were always laughing and telling the latest adult humor. My dad was funny. He was the one who made us (the kids) laugh when we were down. But he really wasn't there for us either. He had other things to deal with that my sisters and I didn't know about until later in life. He was my role model that's for sure. I wanted to be like him. I loved my mother as much, but not in the same sense. She had a problem with control. She was the disciplinarian. I'm sure it stems from a stern Catholic upbringing, because that's what she had known from her step mother. Once she got to slapping or hitting one of us kids, she couldn't stop. She would beat us senseless. Welts and bruises were just a part of it.

I remember hiding from her once as she was beating my older sisters Mary and Linda. When she was done with them, she came looking for me. I was hiding on the bottom shelf of a baby dressing table. I was only about two or three, still living in the house in the city. There was a curtain that hung from the table, covering the shelves, and she was walking back and forth saying, "You can't hide forever!"

I could see the belt swaying right by my head as she paced. I remember it like it was yesterday. But that's where it stops. I don't remember coming out from there though. I am sure that when I did, she beat my ass so bad that I've blocked it from my mind. I probably have quite a few of those memories blocked.

My mother was a madwoman when it came to discipline. I understand now for such a young woman being a wife with all these kids and from where it is she came from; she wasn't ready for, nor knew how to handle, anything! She was on three types of tranquilizers as well! They were prescribed to help her cope with the trauma of her younger brother's death two years after her mom died on the couch. (She was fourteen when her brother accidently hung himself from a tree in their backyard playing cowboys and Indians. She was the only one around and took him down herself.) Mix heavy narcotics, an Italian temper, three jobs, and five kids into your daily routine and see where you sit. She was a wreck. She lashed out at every expense.

I think she almost killed my sister Mary once, and it was over a lie that an eight-year-old neighbor, Amy, made up. Mary was twelve years old. She was babysitting Amy in her mother's apartment that was right across the street from our house. Afterward Amy told my mom that Mary had a boy over. My mom lost it and threw Mary down a flight of steps leading to the basement with a concrete floor. When my mother ran down after her, I thought she would be checking to see if she was ok, nope, that wasn't it. She wasn't done yet. She grabbed Mary by the hair and started banging her head against the floor and a metal support post.

My sister Linda ran to get my Aunt Ava who also lived across the street right next door to the apartment. My Aunt was about 200 lbs. and Linda knew she was the only one who could stop mom. It took every bit of her to do it too. Did I mention that my mother was short? I mean, I told ya she was petite and blonde, but she was real short too. I think four foot ten inches, maybe shorter. Anyway, there was too much yelling and screaming to understand everything that was being said, but I did hear my aunt yelling,

"Her face is blue!" and "she's not breathing!" It was the scariest moment I'd known.

I could go on and on about the abuse, but why? It was a part of our lives that we took as it came. "Take the pain" my life's motto. I was just always glad when the beatings were over. The beating that I just told you about was the last one anyone of us received. I guess it scared my mother. The guilt must have swept through her soul like a frozen shard when she learned that Amy was lying. Can you say "Wake up call"? In my mother's defense I confess that she wasn't like this crazy mad woman all the time. She only went off on us if we warranted it. She didn't know how to control it once someone got her started. We were five brain damaged needy attention starved troubled white trash kids! She had way too much on her plate at a young age. She quit high school in the tenth grade to work, and then started having kids. She was forced into responsibility, a level of responsibility that most people do not endure ever and she had it at age nineteen. She didn't have any time to mature before life kicked in. She lacked intelligence and patience. The biggest thing she didn't have was common sense. With all that being said, how she was able to stop taking all those medications and stop hitting us kids is a miracle. But she did! She gained control of the life she had and handles things with some normalcy.

Back to where I was, (deep breath) I simply was six years old and daydreaming at night in that forsaken trailer.

God, I wanted out of that place. It was so hot it was unbearable. You can't breathe when it's so hot. And In the winter, when it's subzero temperatures and you're living in a trailer, and you have no heat, your bones hurt. You're supposed to keep the faucets dripping in the winter so the pipes don't freeze up. One week after Christmas in that trailer, we had the faucets dripping. My sister Linda had gotten up in the middle of the night and shut them off because the dripping was disturbing her. The pipes froze up; we now had no heat or plumbing.

We were forced to leave and live in our van. (Like the trailer wasn't small enough!) I wanted out of that trailer but I didn't mean this way! So here we were, in the dead of winter, looking for a place to live. We were very unfortunate and had a world of difficulty finding one. To add an even larger burden on my folks, about 4 months into the "van life" my younger sister Ann and I developed tonsillitis and adenoid problems. Back then the doctors only knew to surgically remove the problems. There are alternative methods now.

I don't know how, I knew we didn't have the money but we were placed in the hospital for treatment. It was cold and snowing outside. I remember my folks saying some people were coming up to talk to us from the local newspaper. I was real groggy when they were in the hospital room. I had just come from recovery and the drugs were heavy, but we ended up making the front page with our story. "Family of 7 says NO ONE will rent them a home." I still have the clip. The picture is of me and my sister lying in our hospital beds. My mother was bent over my body, nurturing me. I giggle at the picture when I see it. Not because of the story, but the fashion my parents dawned. My mother had her hair dyed dark and it was teased into an afro. She was wearing a pair of polyester elephant legged pants with a peach silk like scarf that matched her blouse. This was the mid 1970's and the dawn of the disco era. My father was dressed like Mike Brady, the dad on the "Brady Bunch", sitting in a bedside chair next to my sister's bed. We sure didn't have a "Brady" family. I mean, we loved each other and watched out for each other like that, but it certainly was far from normal. I didn't understand why the newspaper was doing a story on us until we were released. When the hospital released us, we had no home to go to. We were living in a 1972, rusty, blue, Ford van. We parked the van in the back parking lot of an AAmco transmission repair shop. This is where my dad worked. The element that bothered me the most is the fact that this building was across the street from a cemetery. Think about the lasting affects those nights had on kids with overactive imaginations. We washed and showered inside the shop after hours. There was no shower, just a place we could hose down, wash up, and rinse. We survived a few months like this. It was a strange time. My sister's and I were able to function at school during this and keep it all a secret. By the time my Parents had some money, the employment, and all the stability to provide for us, they couldn't find a place that we could afford. Looking into the ones we could afford, "Too many kids" they heard. One place told my dad "you can only have up to three kids, but we do accept pets" my dad says, "we'll can I claim two of my kids as pets? We'll just say they are house broken and can speak." She hung up on him.

After the article ran in the paper about us, a flood of calls, hundreds of them! People were offering their spare rooms, motor homes, and basements. We slept in a few basements and jumped from an attic to a family room in some strange man's house for about a month but life for us always worked out, we took the pain and it saw us through the hardest times and eventually we found an actual home that we could rent. And our family was back to where we started, again.

The new place was a three bedroom house. A real house! It had a fire place in the living room. The dining room and kitchen were both actual separate rooms! It had wall to wall green and white floral shag carpet and matching wallpaper throughout. It was hideous but it was ours. Well our place to live anyway. It wasn't a trailer, car, or someone's attic!

In this house, again, my two baby sisters Ann and Marie and I shared a room. But I had my own bed this time. The girls shared another. And again, my two older sisters Mary and Linda had a room to share. The parents got the third room. Still, with this house having tons more room to live than a trailer or van, it only had one bathroom. Five kids and two adults using one bathroom, Things can get nasty if it's not kept clean. We we're really good with it though because we knew what would happen if mom found it unclean. This is the place we were living when that girl Amy lied to my mother about my sister having a boy over to see her while she babysat.

Experiencing life of this caliber had me questioning why anyone would want to have a family.

I said a few times, "I don't want any kids; I don't want a family to support. It's too much to handle, too much pain, too much sadness, too much everything.

It's pretty obvious my folks didn't have the money they needed to provide better, but they made enough to where we survived. My parents didn't do drugs or have substance addictions. They did drink on occasions though. My father had a little battle with drinking for a while when we were young. But then again he was in his early twenties and this was the early seventies. A few marital spats and a broken chair stopped his heavy drinking though. Alcohol never played a role in their relationship again.

Aside from all the chaos, my parents did manage to create a few positive memories for us. They loved parties and dancing. At all the family events we went to... there was always someone playing the old 45 records and everyone else danced. My sisters and I were no exception; we jumped right in with them. I loved dancing. And I was good at it. So was everyone else. Dancing was bonding for us. I cherish every memory from those times.

I won a dance marathon once! It was at a "Moose Lodge". Ever heard of them? Wait.... I'm getting off the subject. I'll finish that story in the next chapter.

Back to the family affair, my mom worked three jobs at times, my dad had two. The times when neither of them had a job are few and far between. I really can't think of one time that ever happened. I have to admit, they fought tooth and nail. We made the best of everything we faced, and we did it together.

Time came to put the past in the past and move forward.

Now that we were stable with a home to call our own, the real problems began to sprout.

At this time, my mother was still beating for disciplinary actions; both her and my father worked their tails off just to meet the ends of critical needs, rent, electricity, food, clothing etc. My sisters and I began to branch out in escape routes from the family chaos. With the eldest child Mary at eleven years old and the permission to venture off to make friends, a few undesirable individuals graced our presence. They offered things that shouldn't be placed in the hands of kids whose minds have not yet completely developed. The lesser of these evils came first.

Chapter 3

Experimentation

I was nine-years-old, now living in a town near Notre Dame University. It wasn't the inner city type like in New England and wasn't the corn fields from where we last lived. When upon that first summer's night at the new house, I was given the invitation to use mind-altering substances. Chuck, a thirteen-year-old boy, who liked my sister Mary, sat with us on the front porch. He held a small white tobacco pipe made of shell or bone.

"Here," he said. "Smoke this. It's called Lebanese Blonde hash. You'll forget all your problems, kid."

He showed me how to smoke it by smoking first. I watched intently as he held the lighter to the hash and lit while he simultaneously drew in the thick white smoke and inhaled. He held it in his lungs for a small amount of time. I counted to ten, and then he blew out a long smooth trail of smoke that billowed up in my face. I didn't mind the smell. So then I followed suit. Well, all except for the smooth exhale of smoke. Mine exhale was more of a cough attack! I hacked a bit and felt my chest burn but it wasn't so bad that it hurt. The effect was elative. I was high, and I seemingly knew how to handle it. Suddenly, my brain could focus. Everything that was so hard to understand before I smoked suddenly became easier to think about. I guess I have what is called an addictive personality. I took to it, as they say, like a fish to water. It calmed my spirit – finally. It hadn't occurred to me until then that I needed something like this to ease the mental anguish. My attempts to emulate how my dad did it hadn't worked. Smoking this did. It helped so much that it took my mind off life I acted like a kid; we ended up playing Hide and Seek the rest of the evening. I felt like a kid for the first time. It was nice.

It wasn't long after when I tried marijuana. This was the best. But being a kid, I didn't stop there: I went through phases of doing whatever new thing I was introduced to, like speed. Barbiturates and Amphetamines were the medical terms for them. Christmas Trees, Yellow Jackets, and Black Beauties were popular pills. I tried Acid; Purple Microdots, Orange Sunshine, and Blotter come to mind in the next years. Most of the speeds only made me feel like a speeding car on triple speed. TRIPLE. I didn't understand how the speed could make me so crazy and the pot would settle me into a feeling of normality like the first time I ever felt safe, relaxed, and clear-headed. I didn't understand anything at the time, not fully, so I kept trying things.

I tried a few beers, but I didn't relate to the affects at all. I had trouble getting past the taste. Can you believe it, a male that didn't take to beer? From what I knew, all men, I mean all of them, drank beer. Funny enough, beer made me more hyper than the speed. I couldn't focus. The effect to me was it made my brain sloppy. I guess it's a chemistry thing.

All of these things were easy to come by: you just had to have the money. Now, in the late 70's at eight and nine-years-old, money doesn't come easy, and when you tend to like this sort of stuff, you have be a bit more creative than Grandma's birthday cards for it. Not like I got any grandma money anyway. Truth being told, if I had received any, I would have spent it on pot.

After learning the terrain of the new area and getting to know a few of the people, I was just walking through an alley behind some houses and three story apartment homes on that block. I came across an elderly couple who were sitting in chairs on the back porch of their five hundred square foot domain. The old guy says, "Hey kid, c'mere." So I went over. He says, "I'll give a buck if ya jump 'at fence and get me suma dem veggies out the garden rightchier'." Do I have to tell you if I did it? I did it alright. I wound up creating my first hustle for cash.

I began going around "raiding gardens." I was stealing fresh vegetables from the backyard gardens of the wealthier neighbors and selling them to old people who couldn't get to the store because of an illness or simply old age. I would go case the gardens to let everyone know what was out there and they were giving me little lists of things they'd like. It worked for all of us.

I was mainly buying marijuana with the money. It's not like I had this elaborate scheme, making money hand over fist. I probably ended up with about twenty dollars a month. But, that did buy enough weed to keep me and my friends high from time to time.

Then of course, I'd get the munchies, so I developed my "stealing phase" from when I was a young boy into a keen habit of kleptomania. My so-called friends said it was a gift I had. (Some gift eh?) I was caught too many times to mention, but I sure did get away with ten times as much. I loved doing the drugs. I hated stealing. However, a nine-year-old kid does not have a lot of adult logic now do they?

Between the drugs and everything I'd wrapped myself up in, I stood clear of my parents. It was a safe place for me. I would get high and my dreams would get bigger and brighter of being richer than thought possible. I will say that I would never suggest that smoking pot should be acceptable behavior during the growth period of one's life. But it was a part of mine. My grades in school were not affected. I did well. Always a good student and studied harder when I was high. I focused better. I began using the high as my creative motivator for just about everything I did. I liked to dance. So I was high when I danced. I loved it. One time, for a small period, I found my way in with a group of kids who would go with their parents to that "Moose Lodge" I began telling you about. The contest I entered was for the Jerry Lewis Telethon. I had to walk around door to door and take pledges from strangers for every hour I danced. I covered about 25 square blocks. The winner got a trophy and the opportunity to present the check to the telethon on the local networks. A chance to be on TV!

The contest ended in a three way tie. It was myself, a bigger kid Jake, who was about 17 years old and dating the grand pooh bah's oldest daughter, and the third person was the grand pooh bah's youngest daughter! We danced for fourteen hours thirty seven minutes! It was incredible. The feeling was exactly like I imagined. Everyone who stayed for the whole dance was cheering and high fiving us! I personally collected $806.00 to donate to the MDA. This was about $500.00 more than the other two.

They presented us with the trophies on the night of the telethon. My mom was proud. She went all out and got me a new suit from Kmart. It was blue with a white shirt. The pants and tie matched too. I felt like a million bucks! My spirits were brought down a big measure when I learned that no one from my family was going to watch me accept my trophy. A few friends and family had traveled in for the Labor Day weekend to barbeque and reunite. They said they would watch for me on the show.

I accepted the award proudly in front of hundreds of strangers at the Moose club and afterwards they drove us to the local news station where we were to present all the money the dance-a-thon raised. There were four of us in all, but the producers informed us that only two presenters could be on the air. I do not know if it was the fact that I brought in more money, or the way I was dressed or what, but the grand pooh bah picked me over his daughter's boyfriend, who by the way was dressed like he was in the cast of Saturday Night Fever, and his own little girl. I didn't care. I wanted to be on TV. And I was.

This was all fun for me and I continued to go to the Friday night dances when the lodge held them. That is until the pioneer rap group "The Sugar Hill Gang" released the song "Rappers Delight" Drastic change occurs here and my life just sped up.

I jumped all of this movement! I loved it! I was drawn to the use of slang and rhyming. I would rap every day about everything. I never thought of doing it like they did and record it. I just liked it a lot. I had a number of talents though. Although dancing was fun, I never thought of being a dancing star. I had some artistic talent. I could draw. I drew pictures of whatever I was seeing; I hadn't the talent to draw from my mind. I thought maybe I could be an artist and become rich. I went with it for a while. I'd smoke some and draw. I wasn't

Van Gogh, but showed a ton of promise with my skills. I'd get high and draw pictures of everything from the Anheuser Busch Eagle to the cover of the TV guide. My parents were surprised how good I was. It didn't last long though. I had friends coming over distracting me all the time. Every time someone came over, I left with them. The artist days were brief. It was on to the next thing in life. At this point, it was Rap. This is the first time I felt I had enough talent to make my dreams come true. I didn't pursue anything right away because I got side tracked. I was introduced to pornography.

Chapter 4

Sex

Like most kids back then, I found Dad's magazines. I took them without guilt and showed my friends. We laughed and poked fun as well as being in awe of the female body. I mean, if there was a heaven, the female body was it for me. Add a joint to that mix, and man, it was bliss. The female body is so curious, is it not? There is so much to explore and learn. How much time do you think it took before I was masturbating? It was before I ever got the first book out of the house! I figured it out real quick. Then something happened that changed me as a person.

I was nine, had just smoked a joint, and was checking out Dad's magazines when my sisters came home. I was going to handle up but since they got there, I had to leave. I went to the apartment building next door. It was a two story tri-plex, with two apartments downstairs and one upstairs. I knew there was a closet under the stairs in that building and that no one was home so that's where I went. It was a tall but small closet. The light bulb swung from a cord in the center of the ceiling and the on switch was a string dangling from the bulb. There was an old three speed bike resting in the corner with one of those rectangular wire grocery carts folded up on top of it. One half of the room was taken up from the ceiling. This room was under the stairwell of the upstairs apartment. So I had to cram myself in to shut the door. I thought for sure I was being as quiet as a mouse until the door flew open and there stood a woman, the single tenant from upstairs. Her name was Cindy. She was a 23 year old very skinny woman. She had large mouth with a huge over bite. And she wore glasses.

"What the hell do you think you're doing?" She embarrassedly asked.

I was like, "Uh I'm standing here holding my dick in one hand and looking at a girlie magazine, what's it look like?"

I didn't say that, but I was thinking it. I slowly straightened myself up by pulling down my shirt to hide my erect member and began to close the book. She grabbed the book from my hand and started looking through it.

I thought, "Oh man, what are my folks are going to do about this?" Cindy closed the book and looked down at my still erect member. Her eyes widened in slight amazement.

"How old are you?" she questioned.

I looked at her knowing I was in trouble and simply said,

"I'm nine."

"You ever seen a real woman naked?" she asked.

"No," I said.

"Do you know what to do with a naked woman?" She asked. Of course I answered yes! She led me upstairs and said what we are about to do I could never tell anyone. It was 1978; I was nine, high on weed, and about to have sex with a twenty-three year old woman. Who would believe me if I did? From that moment on, my perception of what I wanted out of life was altered, forever.

What she did to and with me was more than welcomed. Some people will be offended by that but, I assure you, she did nothing that I didn't want done and let me do things I wanted to know about. Yes, I was young, and these acts were criminal, but I didn't mind. I was already on the wrong path.

She showed me porn films and taught me things I still use to this day to impress women when I'm engaged in sex.

Although I didn't partake nor did she offer, I saw cocaine for the first time. I know the fact that she'd didn't offer me any of it doesn't lessen the offenses of what we were doing but, I wasn't being harmed. I was different. I handled this. Did it scar me? Perhaps on a level I can't comprehend but I certainly have no desire to have sex with under aged children. I like older women!

I found different ways to find my way over to her apartment. We had our little secret. We continued this for the next three years.

I was exposed to so much more of life than just the time I spent with the neighbor upstairs. When I wasn't with her or in school I was busy looking for more. More of whatever it was I found. My veggie stealing days had escalated into breaking and entering. My garden list turned to electronics and patio furniture.

Finding trouble was in my blood. Different friends at different times were searching different aspects of life. We did mischievous things like throwing rocks at the trains that were shipping new cars. At night, banging on the front doors of kids we didn't like in school, then running! It seemed to be funny at the time. I can't make sense of it now.

It was right around this time I saw death. I saw a real dead person.

It was just another bright summer morning. My friend Rich and I were just walking around the neighborhood looking for anything to do to occupy the day. And then the smell hit us, a very strong and very bad smell. It hit us like a wave of heat when you open an oven. It was bad. So we had to find it. We were in front of these homes on a desolate residential street. Not many people lived in these homes. Most were waiting to be demolished. We definitely knew which house the smell was coming from. I was telling him, "Man, someone is dead in here. I know it!" Rich agreed. He just wanted to see it. We covered our faces with our shirts and I followed him in. I felt like I was in a scary movie. I was ready for someone to jump out from somewhere. I just kept my eyes darting all around for any sign of anything. And there he was. A guy who'd killed himself in a closet with a gun. The blood splatter on the closet wall was high. His body was hunched down and forward. I could hardly breathe. I took a good look at him just to say I saw him and got out of there. Rich wanted to call to the police. I did not. We had the most intense conversation. It was full of all the drama two eleven year old kids could muster. And I talked him out of it. I said "We don't want any part of it man! That guy killed himself. We didn't kill him! Let's just get out and let someone else find him!" And we did. We left and didn't say a word. Not to the police anyway. We told a friend or two about it. But nothing legal came our way. I wasn't freaked out by it, seeing the dead guy that is. I don't think it affected Rich either.

My second experience with death was intense.

I was getting high sniffing glue down by the river that ran through town. (I told you I tried everything I could to get high) The river bank was a steep rough sort of mountainous terrain. Fallen trees and unsafe boulders were up and down the bank. There was a make shift path near the base of the bank alongside a wall that edged the river.

I could barely walk I was so high. The state of euphoria that sniffing glue provides has its own identity. I cannot describe the feeling. I'll try though... Being under the influence of toxic fumes makes sounds and visions distorted, not like an acid trip. You don't see things that aren't there, but what you do see is not what it appears.

In my stumbling graze along the river bank path I happened upon a really scraggly looking guy. It was dark but there were some bright lights from across the river. A tire manufacturer had their material yard lights on. I could see the guy clearly. He had long dirty greasy blonde hair; it looked like he had road rash on his face. His clothes were those of dumpster quality.

Obviously he was a junkie. He was sitting there getting ready to shoot up. I said hi but he shushed me and very quickly was setting his arm up with a cord, tying it real tight. He didn't care I was standing there! He just fixed the needle, stuck it in his vein and injected. I stood there not sure if this was real. I watched him untie the cord and lay back. He was lying back on the bank so he was propped up a bit. Then his head fell forward and that's pretty much all he wrote. I watched his body jump around a few times, his breathing was like a wincing sound, like he was breathing sand. And then it stopped. I released a sigh/smirk/ laugh breath in disbelief! I made a comment checking to see if he could hear me but his eyes were rolled up and that was enough for me. I didn't hurry away but, I didn't waste any time getting the hell out of Dodge! I tried my luck at climbing up the bank to get home. I had so much trouble getting up the bank. I started taking deep breaths to clear my head from the glue sniffing. It takes about 15 minutes to regain full senses. I think it took me 30 minutes to reach the top. That was crazy. I wasn't sure what to do. So I went to see the Cindy. I told her everything. She hugged me and laughed a little. She said it was all in my head. "That's what those fumes do to you. They make you see things" and she said "now don't you ever do that stuff again!" Then proceeded to help me out of my clothes and we had sex.

Then Cindy wound up pregnant. BAM! I did not see that one coming! Did you? (Oh yes! the pun is intended...)

Yes, it appeared that puberty had arrived in an alarming way. I was twelve, and had now impregnated a twenty-five year old woman! What the fuck right? But it worked out. How? She started dating a guy from her work and said she would take it from there so no one would find out. Oddly it worked like a charm.

I felt badly about it, but we got out of that jam big time.

You would think that this event would bring our secret to a halt... you are right. It stopped. She went on with her life and I with mine.

My experience with Cindy was enlightening, frightening, and altogether great. I don't know too many boys that would complain about having sex with an older woman. I mean, the other way around, an older man and younger girl is looked at so much more harshly but the violation is the same. I never ever felt I was being violated. I felt I was getting away with something. I thought for sure that I'd get in trouble, I never thought of the consequences though. This was my sexual education. I certainly wasn't told anything at home.

The whole experience with her had helped me mature and see the world through eyes like no other kid my age. Perhaps I was too young, but I was aware of what life was about. It all boiled down to sex and money. I knew that people needed lots of both to make it through life. The question was, how was I going to get it?

Chapter 5

Money

I didn't hide the fact that wanted to be rich and famous.

My parents had different perspectives but equally discouraging. My mother's was demeaning. She literally told me,

"You'll never make it." I argued my points about at least making attempts for it. Her idea of a positive motivational speech was saying, "Prove me wrong then!"

I never understood that. I mean, if you want your kid to do well, shouldn't you make them feel like they *can do it?* But then, my mother didn't actually have the best role models.

My dad's view was like a, "don't even try, you won't have to deal with rejection" kind of mentality. His thoughts for me were really to stay focused in school and you'll get a job that pays you for your brain and not physical attributes. Honestly, from what I saw, he worked, paid his bills, but that's it. My folks couldn't do anything for their kids. Or themselves for that matter! They were barely able to pay rent, keep vehicles, and feed us. There were never any words of planning vacations, saving college funds, or even buying a house, let alone eyeglasses or dental work. My teeth are so messed up. I'm ashamed to speak to strangers because of them. I needed braces in a bad way. There wasn't any money for them. (Take the pain) A girl once told me that she thought I was talking with a mouth full of potatoes or apples until she realized that what she saw were my teeth. I knew I needed something to insure a life where everything like this would be taken care of.

Getting a job using my brain was a choice, but it wasn't going to get me the luxuries that I wanted. I only remember my family going on one vacation, ever … And we had to bring two other family members to help pay for gas. It wasn't like we went to Disney World either. We just visited our relatives in Canada. The desire for being pampered and adored doesn't get satisfied by being a used car salesman or a finance manager; it takes big bucks and lots of friends.

I still wasn't sure how I was going to get there, because I took life as it came, kept my eye on the goal no matter what I was doing.

I think back when, remembering the person I was through different phases. I was a pretty good student and quite popular. I remember being the only fifth grader with a "pot-head" title. Hmm ... think that whole frying your brain thing is a misnomer? I mean I was a 5th grade pothead and making the Honor Roll. It stayed with me through sixth grade as well.

When I made it to seventh grade, I was one of the most popular guys in the whole school. Of course, my two older sisters were already attending that school before I got there, so I had no problems making new friends. The school was a Jr. High school, grades seventh through ninth. But, with the new school, came new problems.

At this point I had been taking karate lessons for a while. My father worked a deal with the instructor at a local dojo. The deal paid the tuition for a few years for me. By the time I made it to seventh grade, I was ready for my black belt.

All new events came about. Here I was, beyond the social intellect of my fellow classmates. I'd been having pornographic sex for three years and about to be somebody's father, already abusing drugs, a little badass with martial arts, keeping good grades, and stepping into the "crimelight" of life. Having popularity was fun, but one needed money to stay there, as well to impress.

I got myself involved with one of my sister's boyfriends, we'll call him Chuck. He was the local dope dealer at a high school just up the road. We had a deal that if I bought the dope, he would sell it, and we would split the profits. I ended up using an opportunity to steal $130.00 from a local church and pulled it off flawlessly. Hey, nobody said that the "crimelight" was a good one to shine. It's not pretty, but there it is.

I gave the money to the dealer and we were in business. It turned into making me $15.00 a day in my pocket and just about all the weed I could smoke. By the third week in school, the word made it through most sources that I was the man to see. Soon after that, I was being pulled in the office by the principal and being searched. I had three nickel-bags of weed in my front pocket when the principle's hand brushed across them. I thought for sure I was busted. It didn't happen though, but it was enough to scare me into giving up my selling days. Chuck was still doing his end of the bargain.

Marijuana, money, and popularity attract girls. I became a target for all the girls who were already sexually active and I took advantage of it. I played along with every girl that came my way. Even the girls that couldn't stand me in elementary school were now coming after me, since their hormones were going crazy and they had heard the rumors.

My want for more money had me constantly thinking of how to make it. Seeing how easy it was to make the fast buck through drugs was cool to me, but I didn't want to go to jail for it. Then, the school gave out boxes of chocolate candy bars to sell. "AHA!" Here was a way to make a load of cash, but the school only gave everyone two boxes each. There were only fifteen bars in each box. I couldn't make any money with that. I broke into the school and ended up stealing twenty boxes that first night. I gave the boxes to another dealer friend, whom will be named Steve, who lived close to my house. I gave him $100.00 to hold them - which he did without hesitation. I sold door-to-door for the next two weeks, after school, and as I walked to and from karate class.

Obviously, my folks hadn't a clue what was really going on. It seemed as if I was selling for the school and turning in the money. Just as I was on the last two boxes, something happened that lead to my first legitimate criminal offense. I went up to a house, as one would normally do in selling door to door. It was hot and I was tired. As I waited for the door to open I put one of the boxes down on the doorstep. The door open and this man started yelling at me.

"Can't you read the sign stupid? It says no soliciting! That means get the fuck outta here! Don't try to sell me nuthin!"

I was a little freaked out by his nature so I took off without saying a word. I got about a half block away when I realized I left the other box of candy bars. I went back to get it. The man had obviously seen it because it was gone. I knocked on the door to ask for it back but he didn't answer.

Under my breath, I said to myself, "shut up. Take the pain; you stole the fucking things in the first place."

I had made enough money to satisfy this ordeal, besides I was sick of walking around. I returned to my friend Steve's house to let him know what happened and that I was finished with this escapade. Steve was pissed about how the guy stole my candy. I told him I was just going to let it go.

"Cest la vie, take the pain." I said.

A few hours later, my sister Linda, her friend Tina, and I were smoking a joint behind my house, when Steve came walking up.

"C'mon you guys, wanna go to the park?" He asked.

We were high, and were probably going to smoke more weed at the park so, what the hell, we went. As we were arriving, we just happened to be passing the place where that guy stole my candy. I immediately told Linda and her Tina what happened. Steve already knew the story, so he walked away from us toward the back of the dwelling. We followed him as he walked up to a dumpster. Oddly enough, there was a container of fuel on top of it. It was Coleman Lantern fuel. And conveniently there was a pack of matches underneath it.

Steve looked and pointed behind us and said, "Hey look at that van."

It was a Volkswagen Van. It was just sitting there rotting. All the windows were knocked out like someone had been throwing rocks through them. Steve told me to open the container and pour it all over the van. I couldn't open it. I had trouble. Steve ended up doing it. He gave me the container and I went to town. I poured it over the top and through the broken windows and all over the paint. He handed me the matches and said, "Here you go, get even." I'll never forget the whoosh and percussion from the flame igniting. It surprised and scared me.

It scared all of us, and we took off running through the park. We ran across a railroad trestle that crossed the river and down along the other side of the riverbank, where we watched the firemen put out what we just started. I never once felt what we did was cool or fun. I remember thinking how the adrenaline from running scared had ruined my high. I didn't really care, but I remember thinking it. We had split up for the walk back to my house.

It didn't matter though because we were spotted doing everything. Ultimately being charged and convicted with arson, I spent the next eight months in a detention center for my involvement. This was the first time I had the opportunity to think about what I had been through so far in my life. It wasn't pretty. I was still only twelve and had dealt with so much. I thought maybe I should write about it all. I decided against that, because I would get a lot of people in trouble. I just figured I should keep the pain inside. I did not however see any harm in doing some creative writing. I quickly learned that I had no problems with writing. I actually loved it. I wrote short stories and poems. I wrote one story about an alien scientist who created the human race and sent us here as an experiment, kind of a theoretical sci-fi explanation of why we are here and alien abductions etc... I titled it "The Human Experiment". I wrote letters to people that didn't exist. I wrote hate mail to people who had wronged me. I apologized to those I wronged. I found that the outlet was a great tool. I never let anyone read what I wrote and when I was released, I just threw it all away. I got out just before Christmas that year.

Chapter 6

Par

The neighbor lady that I was having sex with, Cindy, was about to give birth, and I was back to square one with my dreams of being rich when my parents decided to move because of a major problem with my sister Mary. We were packing up for a state to state move. While I was locked up for the arson charge, Mary was still dating Chuck. He'd gotten her pregnant. She was only fifteen. You see the trend here don't you?

With the family not knowing that Cindy's kid was mine, a ton of attention was on Mary's pregnancy. I believe there was action being taken to negate her child, but Mary had her own plans. She ran away. She stayed gone long enough that it was too late to handle the situation medically. While all that was happening, I got out of the detention center. Like I had said, it was just before Christmas, which is also close to my birthday. So basically, one month after I turned thirteen, Cindy gave birth to my child - unofficially making my mother thirty-one years old and a grandmother. But then, my sister gave birth to her own child two months later making it officially the first-born grandchild. Are you with me? Simply put, my mother was a grandmother of two when she was thirty-one years old, but only knew of one. My dad was thirty-three.

Well to this very day, I've not heard a word from Cindy or the child. My sister's kid is another story! There were plans that his father Chuck would come with us when we moved, but he bailed out. He wanted nothing to do uprooting himself from that town.

My family had set off on the move without me as I had plans to make the trip a few weeks later with a couple friends and their father. A weird thing here, I had a very normal friend, meaning someone who didn't live a life like mine, whose father took him and his younger brother to a different theme park each year during summer breaks. And because he knew I was the only boy in my family and the only friend to his kids, he invited me to join them. He never asked my parents for any money either. He paid everything for me. I went three years in a row with them. I cherish those memories as well. Well it just happened to be a matter of coincidence that his vacation plans were set this year to the exact location where my family planned to move. I just stayed with them until we left on the trip. It was only a couple weeks. I remember crying as my family took off and left me on the steps of the empty house. They all loaded up, packed in, and left. Just like that... and they were down the road. I gave all my sisters hugs. I kissed my mom and told her I'd see her soon. Before I got to my dad they were gone. I never even saw him get in the truck. Man that hurt.

Alas, the move was made, and we settled in to the new place. Outgoing as we kids were, we had no problems meeting new friends. When you're a kid into unsavory activities it's quite easy to find what you're looking for. Especially when you have four sisters!

Honestly, I wanted to give it a go with keeping out of trouble. I figured "a new state and clean slate", no problem.

It's the early 1980's and the new school year started, I'm in the eighth grade, and I'm now in the same grade as my sister Linda as she failed the year prior. I enrolled in a new karate class and found a newspaper route to work after school to pay for it. It was a ten dollar a month community course held in the gym at the Jr. High I was now attending. The paper route was the toughest thing ever. I don't know why, but I am proud of the fact that I am the last of a dead breed. I actually had to carry and walk the newspapers in shoulder strapped double sack. This was an older style fat strapped carrying bag with pockets in front and back. I hated it but I did it. I walked the four and a half mile route after school. I served one hundred eighty customers seven days a week. On Saturdays, I had to walk the route a second time to collect the money the customers owed. My dad helped deliver on Sundays. I would get them ready and in his car, then he drove me on the route at 5:00 a.m. every week. I did the route for a whole year, until I showed my dad that after all was said and done; I only earned nineteen dollars a week. My folks took ten dollars a week for rent! It was teaching me the lesson that you have to pay for everything in life. Well that and my dad needed lunch money! In addition to the paper route I also had household chores to do. Most kids do but, with us, we had a militant regiment of duties. And they would just pop up whenever my mom got a bug stuck in her bottom. If she didn't like the way our clothes were organized in our dresser drawers or closet, she would take all the drawers and dump them out in pile on our beds. Then tell us, "clean it up!" We were all privy to her ways and soon had things the way she wanted when she did her "pop inspection". As we got older and were finding activities to do at different times we weren't always able to finish our assigned chores. We all mastered everything that everyone had to do so in case we needed to trade jobs or something so we could leave and mom would never know who did the work. As long as it was done, mom was fine. Of course my sisters never cut the grass, took out the trash or raked leaves. Those were always mine.

Before my fourteenth birthday, and now in ninth grade, a freshman in high school, I continued my martial arts training and my sister Linda and I got a job at major fast food chain. Minimum wage was $3.35 an hour. We both entered the "work experience" program available through the school. We were released from classes at 11:30am and went to work. It wasn't long before my Linda dropped out of school and quit the job, but I hung in there. I was always a great student, and no matter what I was going through, I never failed a grade and had a job.

I worked at a restaurant four miles from the school and had to walk to get there. And because of the McDonald Act of 1963 any student under the age of sixteen wasn't allowed to work more than three hours a day. So, after four hours of school, a four mile walk to work, then three hours of shelling out burgers and fries, I had a six-mile hike home. I did it every day. No problems. The paper route trained me for this. But … and this is a big but, I had graduated from smoking weed and taking pills to snorting cocaine.

Cocaine was a big part of the next six years. Crack, Powder, and Paste! Between my ego trip with being popular and my addictive personality, this drug, all forms of it, was the worst thing for me. I flew by the seat of my pants through this era. It was fast and high – constantly. And nothing good came from it. I was selling it through the drive thru window at work. I had stolen a few cars and robbed a few homes without ever getting caught. I was caught one time for stealing some fishing gear from a neighbor's boat he had parked alongside his home. I wasn't caught in the act though. I gave the stuff to a friend and he pawned it. He was caught through the pawn shop and ratted me out as the culprit. I was charged with grand theft. I didn't get locked up for it though. I was fifteen, an A B student, and had a job. Probation was the sentence. That is what happens to first offenders that do wrong but not worthy of taking up a bed in the county jail. For a fee of course, it's called Cost of Supervision. This was my second stint with probation so I knew the ropes. I completed this term without incident. But I wasn't finished with drug use, or the antics.

To graduate at the top of my class as a criminal I committed armed robbery. Yeah, I was freaking out that night! I worked at the taco restaurant I robbed. I took the night off, so I could party with a girl I knew from school. We were partying in my parent's neighbor's shed! No one knew we were there. About 11:30p.m, we ran out of cocaine. I knew where to get more but had no money. I left the girl alone, so I could go get more. I considered getting some fronted to me from my dealer but I really hated having to owe anyone anything. I found myself waiting outside the restaurant, my place of employment. It was closed but I knew they still had to make the bank deposit. The guy who covered for me that night, and the manager exited the building and headed for their car. I walked up to them and I robbed them at gun point. A. 357 I "borrowed" from my uncle's house. They both were in shock. I never made eye contact with either of them.

I just kept holding the gun up and grabbing for the bank bag. My friend was asking me calmly, "Hey man what are you doing this for? Roy! What's wrong with you? Just stop man!" I got the bag from the manager's hand and ran! I never looked back. I just ran. I wasn't scared, though my conscience struck me hard with guilt. The fear I just put my coworkers through was horrible. I knew I was going to jail for this. But that's what cocaine use does to you, it takes away the logic. And the rest of this night didn't make any sense either. I took the money, bought more cocaine and that girl and I snorted it all.

Eventually the night had to come to a close and I still had the gun. I was going to put it back, but 4 o'clock in the morning is not a good time to be returning an uncle's .357 under his mattress! So, I just put it on the floorboard of my mother's car. I do not know why. I think I just didn't want to have it with me. I didn't realize my mom would be leaving for work at 5am. Eeeeek! (Sorry mom.) I'm glad I wasn't there when the police pulled her over.

The shorter version of the fiasco went like this: I turned myself in for the crime I'd committed. I was sent to a mini prison for about fifteen months, I got out, and had to serve more time on probation, correction, this was parole now. It's the same thing as probation but a lot more involved with your daily life and it's more expensive.

While serving this stint of exterior incarceration, I had a sexual affair with my parole officer. Wait… what? Yeah. I had one of those inappropriate parole officer/parolee affairs. Look, it happened, what can I say? I love sex and I love women. I also love a bit of risk. It's an adrenalin rush. Anyway, she was a freak. She came on to me a few times before I caved in. I wanted to jump in when she first gave me a hint and a wink but I was figuring it being some kind of trap. I finally jumped when she made an unannounced visit to surprise me at home. What she did when she locked the door didn't surprise me. But it would you! So I'll refrain from giving you the details. But here I was again, another boy toy. It didn't bother me that she was engaged either. She wasn't married yet and I had plenty of experience with having secret sex so I went with it.

We partied with every drug out there and always wound up like we were filming a pornographic movie. We had sex in the probation office once but that was way too risky so that was just once. It was real fun for a couple years until I started getting close to finish my term. I was out on four years parole with a special condition in my favor. I was supposed to get released after two years if I completed a few conditions. I did them and when I brought it up about being released, she refused. She wanted to keep me at her beck and call. I told her I would go over her head and she said she'd violate me first. Of course I fired back with the ability I have of mentioning how she was fixing drug tests and the fact that she's been banging a case number. This argument was at her parents' house, in their bed! Well I got dressed and stormed out saying "you do what you gotta do, and I'll respond."

She thought she was being clever by waiting eight months for her system to dry out and get all her affairs in order before she posted my picture in the local paper's "county's most wanted" section. The post read "POLICE SEEKING SUSPECT", the charge was "violation of parole for armed robbery" That definitely freaked me out.

The night before the picture was posted I went out on a really cool date with a girl I'd wanted to go out with. It was a great date. She came home with me as well and even spent the night. We were woken by someone beating on my front door. I open it to find a good neighbor of mine holding the morning newspaper in my face. Ever see your picture in the paper on the wanted list? Never thought I would. But here it was! How does a woman respond when she wakes up in a guy's bed with whom she'd just had sex, on their first date I might add, and see his picture in the newspaper as a "wanted" felon? To my surprise it wasn't like she panicked or knocked stuff over gathering her things to rush out the door. She was calm. I quickly explained the story. She understood that people get into trouble for stupid things but of course she wanted to stand clear of the immediate event! Before she left she gave me a small peck on the cheek. She said, "You're cute, intelligent, and funny. I see a drive in you to be what you set out to be. But the situation you have yourself in tells me that you place focus on the wrong things in your journey." And she left.

I called the police and said that I'm the guy in the paper and wanted to turn myself in. He was like, "eh ahh well its Labor Day weekend and unless you wanna sit in jail til Tuesday for court, don't. Just lay low and come in then…"
So that's what I did.

I went to a friend who was having a barbecue, hung out and I enjoyed myself because I knew I was going back to jail. I wasn't worried about it though. I can handle it. I knew that day would come eventually. I also knew I would be able to retaliate on my probation officer. I would give them all the details. And did they? I held nothing back. Things she didn't think I knew, I told them. She had no counter or answers for them therefore she lost her career and all her credentials in that field. I just simply had to live in jail for another short period of time. I guess she didn't think I could take the pain. Take the pain… That's what I do best.

Chapter 7

Hello Fame... Syke!

I was about nineteen, almost twenty returned to jail this time I served eight months flat time. I finished the sentence out, what is called, "day to day" so I wouldn't have to be back on parole. I attempted writing a screenplay while locked up this time. I called it "CARTS." It stood for Con Artists, Robbers, and Thieves. When I got out, I wrote another screenplay called, "Demented Youth;"

I didn't want any more trouble, so I created a barrage of activities to do with trying to make these screenplays happen. I loved break- dancing back in the day and the genre of music from it, so my Cuban friend Manny and I started a mobile disc jockey service. We called ourselves the MBDJ's. (Master Blastin Disc Jockeys) The screenplay stuff took a backseat to this. I knew to hold on to them in case I was successful at any phase.

I was really enjoying the disc jockey field. It was so much fun! Manny would spin and mix. I could rap and choreograph well. We really performed shows instead of just playing music. I became real comfortable behind a microphone. My natural sense of keeping an event lively in a comedic style earned me a night at a local comedy club's "open mic night." But, this was a contest for a radio station. The winner got $987.00 and a chance to come back the following week to try again. I won eleven weeks in a row! WOW! Here was my door to everything I'd always dreamed.

I had a stage name already planned out. I took my mother's maiden name because it was already internationally famous and I heard that is how the rock band Van Halen got their name. It was a tribute to their mother. I liked that so I followed suit.

After winning each week I received a check with my stage name on it. I kept saving them and said I would cash them all together as soon as I lost. Problem, I could not cash these checks. I had no true ID for the name. I had to get legal. I had to go to court, pay a fee, and change my name, that is, if I wanted to keep earning this money.

Changing my name caused an emotional ripple with my father. I'm his only son and I changed his last name to my mother's maiden name

I explained to my dad, "Look at it like this, first, if I fuck up in Hollywood, it'll be mom's name that gets dragged through the mud, and second, it's not like you think I have a chance to make it out there anyway."

I felt my Dad's disappointment when I chose this avenue. He really wanted me to be a "suit" in the business world. I had been working a real job, on the books, since I was nine years old. I did a lot of things for work trying to stay legit. Besides the five years at the fast food chains, I worked at a dog spa for a bit. I was bathing and flea dipping pets. I don't like working with animals. That's what I learned from that job. I detailed cars working with my dad. My dad didn't detail them; he was a salesman or manager of a car lot and got me the job. I learned a great money making trade right here. Do a great job, people will tip you and then call you back to do it again. It's very lucrative for a motivated individual. I took mega pride in my work. I guess my mom's eccentricities with organizing and her "mommy dearest" cleaning frenzies helped out there. (thank you mom) I was so good I went into business for myself. "Attention to Detail" was the name of my little mobile auto detail company. My dad also got me a job when he left the auto industry and returned to being a carpenter. He worked his way up through a contractor company and when he was lead foremen, he hired me onto a crew. I worked with that for a few years, as well as continued with my detailing. I have to admit, I loved it. I learned as much as I could from the best carpenters. "Great trade to fall back on if I ever get into a bind later on in life" is what I heard from everyone. But it didn't feel like work to me. Building houses was great physical activity. I loved the attitude and comradely ways of the guys. I grew up always surrounded by women. My whole life! Besides the times of being incarcerated I was never around a group of guys for lengthy periods. This was great. This was awesome! The guys were rude and always cutting up. And god forbid if anyone acted weak in any way. Carpenter crews will chew you up and spit you out! One has to be mentally and physically tougher in this field than those that are flipping burgers. Learning how to build intrigued me at every level. I felt I would spend the rest of my life constructing anything dreamed. I wanted to make everything out of wood. Things like lawn chairs and firewood bins etc. A point to make here is I never earned much money. Even though it was now a part of me, it simply covered the basics. Rent, food, lights, phone gas, car, insurance, the list keeps going! No matter how good I got at anything, I never seemed to earn big money. It seemed I was always broke. And next thing I knew was here was $10k in checks for telling jokes? Failure, to me, is not being able to make enough money to support you with all the essentials of life and then some! Success, to me, is being able to not worry about any bills, EVER! Having enough money in the bank to eat, drink, be merry, and the privilege to live life at your pace, at your discretion. Now I'm not saying if you are not able to do this yourself that you are a failure. Not in the least. I'm saying that this is my failure. It's my goal to succeed financially to do this. You are only a failure if you don't achieve the goals you set for yourselves. I heard someone say once, "You only fail if you don't try" HA! Not true. "You won't succeed if you DON'T try." Yes, logically that is true. You won't know if you don't try. But if you do try and do not get the outcome that you had in mind, then that is a failure. For me, failing here was returning to the job that just paid my bills.....

After making the decision to go for it with comedy I signed a deal to make $15k in just six weeks. I felt a surge of positive energy and it kept rising. I met a few people pretty quick. There was a man and woman couple that liked my show. They stayed to meet me after. We hung out and joked a while. They got to know me a little. Then they'd invited me into their bedroom. We had a few threesomes. They were really nice. They listened to a few of my ideas. After I let them read one of my screenplays they said they wanted to help me move my career. He had a small connection with someone in Hollywood. His brother-in-law was a VP at a film company. After a few calls and conversations, the VP flew in to meet me. We talked shop over lunch. He thumbed through the script. He mentioned, "for the most part" the script would get changed due to the amateurish writing style but wanted me to fly out to LA for a presentation. I did so and it went well. They offered to buy the script but, had no use for me per say. I wanted to be in the film. It's the reason I wrote it! I was on this road chasing my dreams. Everything I'd overcome to get to the window of opportunity and they did not want me, only what I had. I did have an attorney and he was in on the meeting via speaker phone. When the meeting finished my lawyer had me take him off the speaker and to me only he said "It's all on the table, take the money or thank them kindly for the offer and their time but gracefully decline."

I declined because I had faith I was going to make it and I would produce this film independently. I flew back home and found myself talking to my dad about it. He was more than happy to rub my face in it.

First thing he said was, "I told you so."

I said, "Dad I almost made it."

He said, "Almost don't count."

I said, "I know, but they did want my script!"

I knew I had something. So why not make it myself? I was now on a mission.

Moving right along, still about twenty years old I wound up living with a roommate I'd met through friends of my baby sister Marie. Her name was Karen. She was an overweight, unattractive girl who wanted a relationship with me in a bad way. Karen was the kind of girl that sucked attention out of the room by her negative energy though. She was short, pudgy, and deprived of a clear completion. I know... it's for some people, but she just didn't turn me on. Maybe if she emanated a more positive energy? I don't know.

What made it so difficult was the fact that we worked together too. Before I really got the sense of how she was she had helped me gain employment with the cable locating company where she worked. I was out in the field and she worked the office. This was a cake job. It was great money too. But I messed that all up taking too much time off doing comedy shows. Anyway Karen and I were not compatible as roommates let alone engaging in a relationship. She was practically relentless with the pleading and these "moments planned" for us. I booked myself at all the local and circuit comedy clubs around the state to just stay away from her. The problem occurring with this is she always found a way to come to the shows! I was hiding behind stuff at the "after parties" so she would think I left...

I actually agreed to the most bizarre favor ever asked of me to keep away from this girl. I ran into an ex-girlfriend in the grocery story one day. Wanda. I hadn't seen height nor hair of her in over two years. She was with a boyfriend. The guy looked okay. He was a little old for her I thought, but, "What the heck, ain't my life!" We kept in touch for a few weeks, and then the two of them asked me to dinner one night. After the meal they just flat out asked me if I would impregnate her!

The whole "you have good genes" song and dance was in play... They had an elaborate detailed plan of how things would go. They actually wanted me to do this the old fashioned way too! I remembered she was a little freak so what the hell, right? He wasn't going to be involved or anything, just the Wanda and I. It wasn't that long until it worked. She was pregnant after the third attempt. However, it wasn't the most pleasant experiences. There wasn't a connection. I felt that if the goal of creating a life takes precedence over an orgasm the body reacts differently. If the goal of just having the most erotic sexual encounter is removed, it is replaced with uncomfortable silences. It was definitely the most awkward sex I've ever had. But we were successful.

Seemingly things were fine for the next four or five months with the two of them. I got a few calls saying hello and updates. It was all cool. Her man had money, she was driving a new BMW and I know she couldn't afford it.

Like most bad situations that occur, Wanda had one hit her from left field, from under the bleachers! I'll explain.

When she was in her sixth month, Mr. Money Man dumps her. As it became abruptly clear, he was gay. The way he informed her was quite different than just sitting someone down and saying...." I'm gay". No, nothing like that. He drove her to a state in the "deep south", checked into a not so seedy but still had a "creep" factor motel, and waited for his lover of fifteen years to be released from prison. His lover was getting out after a three year sentence for a car accident that was his fault where someone died. The two of them set it up so where Wanda would learn what she's getting into by trial and error. They put on a show for her! (I told you she was a freak) but, apparently she wasn't that much of a freak because she would have no part of it! She would rather be a single mom. She never asked me to step in even though I was the father. She never wanted to tie me up like that. She understood the road I was on. She wanted a baby more than she wanted a man. She had the ability to do this. Mr. "Moneybags" had put her through Cosmetology school, and she was a working stylist. On the day she was telling me the story of what happened at the motel with the two guys, she was cutting my hair. We were at the apartment where I was rooming with Karen. Then there's a knock at the door. It's a girl from my past.

Her name was Sally. I met this chick through some hillbilly drywall hangers that I met through my dad's construction employment. She was one of the wives' little sister. The girl was from the "deep south" too. She was about 18 and was visiting to party. They knew I partied hard, so they hooked us up. And did we ever! We partied the whole week she was there. Then she left. But here she was again, at my door. "Oh my god" I said. "How did you know to find me here?" She had tracked me down through a restaurant I took her to a couple times during our little party week. My mom worked there. And was still working there when she came looking. My mom gave her directions to my location.

Sally was holding an eighteen month old child that yes, was mine. We took the tests. Definitely mine, but she was not there for anymore than just to introduce her son to his father. She didn't want anything from me either. Sally told Wendy and I that when she learned she was pregnant, her mother said they would raise him together. They had in their minds that a day would come to introduce us just for the sake of saying that we did meet. This was that time.

Sally's mother moved to the town next to mine after the child was born. Not by any true meaning, just coincidence. Sally remained living in the deep south until she could travel with him. He was just a normal toddler; he understood what no meant, so she made the trip. I asked her to take some time to really get to know me. I said, "Hey, you never know." This is where I actually felt the reality of someone depending on me for the first time. I attempted to grow up.

As the following five weeks passed I learned about the kind of person Sally was. I actually couldn't believe the views of this girl. Born and raised in the backwoods is scary. She lived in an old camper top (the kind that goes into the back of a pick-up truck) and it was up on blocks in a wooded area on a family member's land. Talk about back woods! The running water was the creek that ran through the land. Food was kept in old nasty beer coolers. Unless it's a kill, then it's kept away from camp. There was a generator to power up a few of the campers there, but only at night. Apparently they had a little family village living there. I was baffled by how dumb she was too. She said something to the effect of only making it to the fourth grade when they moved to the hills.

I couldn't believe it. I certainly thought about me having a son being brought up in that environment. I set my mind to do the right thing. And before we had a chance to do anything like look for an apartment or find her a job I went over to see her and when I got there...nothing. I knocked on her mother's door and she didn't answer. I walked to the back of the house thinking maybe they were back there. And he was. The boy was there, playing in the dirt. He was filthy and standing there in just a diaper. He had about twenty insect bites on him. I yelled for Sally but got no response. So I brought the kid inside to clean him off. I had time to wash and change him before I heard some thumping in the celling. I realized then that Sally was up in the attic. No wonder why she didn't hear me and the kid was outside alone. I found the attic door. A step ladder was there that she'd used to climb up. I climbed and popped my head up expecting to see her pillaging through her mother's storage. Nope. She was with a black man. They were naked and she was on top of him in the sitting position. She wasn't jumping up and down when my eyes first focused on the situation. She was too busy lighting the crack cocaine in the glass pipe she was smoking!

What do ya do? What do I do? Well I'll tell you what I did; I jumped down, grabbed the kid's car seat and baby bag, put him in my car and went home. Of course I knew they would come running but her and her mom called the police. I didn't think they would, considering the circumstances. The Sheriff's Department answered the call. They arrived at my place like I kidnapped the kid. I had to stand out in the front of my house with my hands in the air, all the neighbors running out looking at what's going on. Again, this was crazy. Obviously I was given the opportunity to explain, but the child had her last name. I had to give him back. I don't know how things would have turned out had I been allowed to raise him. But I'm 1000% positive it would have been 1000% better than what he got. I didn't go to jail for this. I actually placed a complaint legally about her but before anyone got anywhere with it she went back to the backwoods. I was told that she was last seen hitch hiking in shorts and no shoes out of town. I believed it.

I started hearing the "you should write a book about your life" from people who I had time to get to know long enough to fill them in on this much of my life. My thoughts were all for it. If it would make me rich, I'd do it. Then, I thought "who wants to read a book about some guy dealing with some shit?" I mean, everybody goes through some shit, right? If there's a choice of reading about a Hollywood celebrity or some guy... most people will want the star. If I wasn't writing to help me cope with doing time I found I had no use for writing. And with me already failing at the writing thing, I just saw fit to move on. Besides I had no time for it. I wrote jokes constantly for my act.

Chapter 8

Women, the Road, and Hard Time...

I had to sit back and reflect. Neither woman, who'd mothered a child from me, wanted me. The one chick that did want me, Karen, looked like a cross between William Shatner and James Earl Jones and made me miserable! I had to get the hell out of there and hit the road. I can find women all over. Any man can always find a woman. It's written in the small print in the "Man Card Handbook". It doesn't matter what you look like or how you act, if you have a lot of money to spend foolishly, you will find a woman. Now if you don't have the money, well then that's when it matters who you are and how you act. I certainly had enough of the "family life" scare. I just went in to the next lane on my road from rags to riches. I switched gears, put the hammer down, and drove.

I had a little money at this point earning interest and enough coming in to give me a taste of my dreams, so I went for it. I took my act to the next level. I got lucky having the opportunity to meet and work with an idol of mine. Sean Kensington. Sean was an "off the wall" comedian. He was a very successful entertainer and took a liking to me. He took me under his wing and allowed me to be the first of two opening acts for him on a national tour. I was paid the most money I've ever earned. I learned everything I could about the business in between all the partying after every show. It was a lot too; a big venue, small clubs, doing two sets a night in some places. I had to step away almost as fast as I jumped on board. The tour was for forty weeks. I made it to the thirty first week's shows, and quit.

I was back to using cocaine. I was clear of any responsibilities to a family life so I simply started again. I kicked into heavy use because of the abundance of it and wanting to keep up with the people I was partying with. But I came too close to doing too much too many times. I was twenty years old. I didn't want to die. So I quit. I quit the drugs. I quit the tour. I just quit. I was on the biggest stage of my life, only to see bigger stages later, and I quit.

I felt I had made a name for myself on the tour. I could drop a few names now and perhaps get a contract. The thoughts about what would happen if I failed did creep from the back of my mind.

"Almost Don't Count." I could hear my dad saying already. And I'll be damned if he wasn't right!

All I accomplished by quitting the tour was damaging my name with some people who were helping me. No, that's not true. It's not the only thing that was achieved. I don't believe I'd be alive if I kept the pace and stayed. I am alive now. I saved my own life. I did the right thing. They say you live and learn. My accent is on "YOU LIVE"

I began giving it my best on the journey, only to meet its demise at the same time.

I was fortunate enough though to have established my name as a local favorite in the small local circuit clubs. Those clubs dealt with so many comedians they didn't know one from the other. They didn't care about resumes. As long as every seat was filled, the owners were fine. A year or so of keeping focused on my goals I woke up in a very bad relationship with a Columbian stripper. Marla. This chick was completely insane. She was the product of incest. Her parents were uncle and niece. When they married each other in Venezuela, their family disapproved and kicked them out. They came to America and raised Marla. To give you an inkling of how insane Marla was I'll tell you this. Whenever we visited her parents it was always at a restaurant. They wouldn't let Marla know where they lived. They never said why but they did share the story of how they forced her into life. When Marla was seventeen years old her parents sent her on a two week vacation somewhere. When she returned she found all of her belongings packed on the porch and everything else was gone. They had moved. And they never let her know where they lived! This was five years later and she still didn't know. I now understood the restaurants.

With knowing all this I figured leaving her was the only answer and I left her. I had befriended one of the bouncers at the strip club where Marla worked. He was a short frumpy dumpy guy that had a secret at the club. He was a doctor for his day job. He owned two popular family practice centers. Dr. Vernon was the epitome of depression. He knew he looked like the world's tallest troll. He stood about 5'9" and had a "Santa" face. It was covered with a patchy salt and pepper beard. He tried to grow his hair long but he lost all the hair on the top. There wasn't even enough to attempt a comb over. He had this really big swollen beer belly but really short skinny legs, like a standing bullfrog. His depression turned him into a sort of functioning junkie. He was addicted to a drug called NuBain. I think it's a synthetic morphine. He would do what is called "skin popping". He wasn't injecting it into a vein, just anywhere else on his body that was usually covered by his clothes. I did watch him shoot up some Jack Daniels whiskey into a vein one time! That turned out to be a bad night. Of course I didn't learn all this about him until I moved in with him as a roommate. Vern never hid the fact that he worked at the strip club for the sole reason of being able to meet the girls. Because of his appearance, he wasn't approached by any females. But if they had to work with him they could meet and see him as a real guy. It actually worked which is why I don't think he ever stalked or killed anyone. If there was ever anyone destined to be a stalker, Vern was the one. He had an infatuation for guns. He wore a double shoulder holster that held three weapons. An old 44 magnum, a .9mm, and a desert eagle 50mm. It was sick. He was sick. Besides his depression and his addiction to NuBain, which he spent in the tune of about fifteen thousand dollars a month, He had adopted a stripper! He fell in love with one of the girls from the club. He said he would do anything he could to have her as a part of his life. Just to talk and hang out, never any sex. It was a strictly platonic affair. He just wanted to take care of her. She even had a boyfriend. He spent hundreds of thousands of dollars on her. He made sure her and her boyfriend wanted for nothing. They got new clothes whenever they passed a mall, for them both. Needed new cars? No problem. Needed a house? They got one!

While all this was going on I was still working the comedy circuit with my act and writing my ass off. I believe I wrote my masterpiece during this time. It was a heavy metal comedy show.

Then I met another girl who changed my entire perception of life, again!

We met; she introduced herself as Tracy Lords. "Holmes, John Holmes" was my response. We laughed and it went from there. Tammy was her real name. We had a few dates, got passed the "Who do you know in this town?" stuff. Spent a few nights at her place, she spent a few at mine. I really dug the way we were so compatible. Without haste, I packed my stuff from Vern's and found a quaint little one bedroom place. And just like that, we were living together. She liked the attention I got in public. She wanted it as much as I did. She agreed to go on a national TV talk show and talk about having sex in public! That was a trip I'll never forget. The whole time I was working angles trying to make a wave with anyone of importance back stage. Then I put on an even bigger act for the show! I got a few calls and a few extra gigs but nothing came of it. (Fail.)

I kicked it in gear with getting the production together for my new show. I was the writing songs and performing stand-up now with a heavy metal band. "The Rockin' Joke Showcase" was the masterpiece that was going to propel my career. The slogan was "Rock 'em if they can't take a joke." We needed a few hundred thousand dollars to get this off the ground. I booked as many shows as I could and worked odd jobs while raising money. I almost had the money, but, almost does not count.

My new awesome girlfriend even tried helping with my goal! I booked a stand-up tour along the southern states because this was the winter months. I set up the six week run to finish in Galveston Texas, where Tammy grew up. Her parents still lived there. I figured we could visit them, perhaps at least go to dinner. Well, Dr. Vern was more than happy to make the 1100 mile drive with Tammy to pick me up. So they did. They took turns driving. I thought she was going to fly in and just rent a car to pick me up. Then after the visit we would fly home together. I was surprised to see both of them there.

As I finished my third and final show that last night, I said goodbye to a few of the other comics I knew and walked outside. I smelled weed in the air as soon as we exited the building. I mentioned it. "mmm" I said. "You guys smell that? Somebody's burning some green" The smell got stronger as we approached Dr. Vern's truck. That's when they proceeded to tell me about the detour they made to visit a friend of hers that she had grown up with where they purchased one hundred sixty pounds of marijuana at an unbelievable low rate. Vern then explains that he's three quarters of a million dollars in debt and he needed a quick sure fire way to turn big cash. I was pissed when I saw the weed and heard the plan. I was trying to be legit. I yelled at them. "Do y'all have any idea what happens if we get caught?" They were going to sell it back home and would've made a small fortune. But certainly not enough to make $750,000.00! Oh, but they were hoping to make the trip at least once a month! Not really sure what I was doing but I was furious and made another bad decision. I decided to drive back with Vern and make Tammy fly home. I was tired already and now had this situation on my hands. Even though I knew the consequences I still stayed with the truck. I was so angry I guess I wanted the time to scream at Vern for this. I guess I never thought we'd get caught.

We dropped Tammy off at the airport after of booking her a flight. I made a call to my sister Linda to pick her up when she got home. Then the drive began.

Since it was Dr. Vern's truck, his stuff, he was driving the whole 1100 miles back home.

After three hours of paranoia, handling travel details for Tammy and freaking out on Vern, I went to sleep in the backseat. I took off my jeans and just covered up with a towel I had. I couldn't stretch out on the floor. Vern did the best he could to conceal the pot. He packed it all in coolers. You couldn't smell it anymore but there were a few more coolers than you'd normally see from just two guys traveling state to state.

Two and a half hours after we left, we were pulled over for speeding. I woke up to lights and badges. I was real dazed but saw Dr. Vern throw it into park and he mumbled something about, "don't worry, I'll handle this", and got out. He walked back to the police. I gained my senses of the situation. I very quickly put my pants back on and started looking out the windows. There were two cars and three of four cops already there before I finished.

"Man! There's no way out!" I thought.

Instantly I knew I was going back to prison. I thought of my girlfriend. I loved her. I thought of my career. It's over, no matter what. The thoughts of my life and future went running ramped. It's the worst I've ever felt.

A narcotic detective opened the door by my seat and had me "step out of the vehicle". He had Dr. Vern and I stand on the side of the highway facing the front of the truck from about twenty feet away while they searched. The headlights were blinding as I tried to watch the police dog that was called to the scene. I could barely see him. I saw a shadow of fur jumping up on the side of the truck. I think it was a young Golden Retriever. He was on a leash and was lead to each section of the vehicle. I don't know what he did to signal but it wasn't difficult to look through the windows and see the 10 large coolers sitting nice and uniform in the back. You'd have to be a special kind of stupid to not inquire about them.

Vern started speaking, "Dude, you gotta take this for me. You gotta! I have a ton of money to get you out, but I can't from inside." He followed it with, "Tammy is going to freak! She is my accomplice. If there's any time to serve I'll do it but I can't go to jail right now!"

I didn't want Tammy to go to jail. I didn't want her to have anything to do with this at all! Obviously, that's the very reason I put her on the flight. If I hadn't witnessed the financial aspect of Vern's life with my own eyes I would have never even considered saying it was my marijuana. But I saw how much he had. Everything was going so fast. I had zero seconds to think of all the repercussions so I took it. I took the rap. I said it was all mine.

The police walked us to the back of the truck where there were now about eight officers from several squad cars. It was asked by the detective on scene, "what do we have here gentlemen?" I said, "What we have here is failure to communicate!" I got a few laughs... But as soon as the moment passed I said with all sincerity, "Sir, this is one hundred sixty pounds of marijuana. I bought it in the last town we were in and Dr. Vern knows nothing. I was using him for this run and he didn't know it." I looked at Vern and apologized. They handcuffed me a placed me in the front seat of a really nice undercover Iroc Z. The detective got in the driver's seat and shut the door. He began talking to me right away. He asked about the "real" story. I said, "Man, I said what I said and that's all I'm saying." He retorted with, "Well then you're going to prison my friend." "You're not my friend." was my reply. He said, "C'mon man, you can't expect me to believe to a twenty two year old kid paid for all that weed. Where'd you get the money?" "I saved it up" I said with a sarcastic undertone. "And you got all that marijuana into that truck without your friend knowing?" That was a good question. Logically it was difficult to believe someone could put that much of anything in someone's vehicle without them knowing, but I was sticking to my guns. My voiced quivered when I answered, "Did you ever have one of those friends you'd do anything for?" He said, "Yes!", as his voice raised an octave. "But not one I would go to prison for." I retorted with, "That's why you could never be my friend". This was the late 1980's and I wasn't aware of the mounted video cameras on the dash board. This was all recorded.

I just felt there was a way past all this, especially because Dr. Vern was going to pay for all the legal bills. I would have a hired defense team. All I ever had was public defenders. I was always guilty, but still, public defenders just want to get through the day. They don't work for your case. They just get it off the desk.

I was read my rights and arrested, Dr. Vernon wasn't. The last time I saw him I was looking at him through the food tray opening of a solid metal "holding cell" door at the police station. I could just see his eyes and could barely hear him talk. He was saying, "Don't worry bro, I am going to get you out." And that was it. I never saw him again. There was news of him from time to time. I'll tell you about it later.

Tammy never took the flight home like she was supposed to. My bail was set at $100,000.00 So I needed $10,000.00. It took her four days to make my bail money and we took a bus home. We both knew what was going to happen from here. But we were "in love" and no matter what; we were going to get passed this together. (Sound familiar?)

Court dates had come and gone. I did everything I could to prolong my sentence, including marrying Tammy, but it was inevitable. I was charged with Felony Drug Trafficking of Schedule II narcotics. It turned out to be 158.8 pounds not 160. It did not matter though. I went back to prison. This time, I was a second offender. For whatever reason, maybe they didn't have my criminal records but this charge went in the books as a first offense. I was lucky and only got five years.

Before I knew it, I woke up in a penitentiary in the Deep South. I wondered if this is where Wanda's boyfriend's boyfriend did his time. Nahhh, that was in a different Deep South state.

Things went wrong from the start inside. The first day, after completing the inmate orientation, we were being walked to our bunks. "The Walk", the walk is the 1000 foot entry way that you will only ever use once. It's the way in. Its path leads from the rear of the Main building to the general population rec yard. It's just a sidewalk that has a fenced cage around it. The fence stops but the sidewalk continues for another few hundred feet to a center point of the rec yard, and then a few sidewalks branch from there to other parts of the prison. As the new inmates are brought in, just like you see in the movies, it's quite the spectacle. Everyone gathers around and points out who's the scared one, who's a seasoned inmate, but mostly they want are looking for old friends. There are a lot of guys checking to see if any of them look gay, or sweet enough to turn gay. The yelling, screaming, and laughing that occur during this walk are insane.

There were forty-one new inmates coming in with me on my first day. We were given state issued clothes and what not, and had to carry them in our arms like we were bringing someone a birthday cake with lit candles. We had to walk in pairs so they could count us evenly. If you mess up, you get sent to the "cell block". "The hole", Solitary confinement for those not keen with prison terms.

I was keeping my head up and doing the normal tough guy attitude walk just wanting to get this time over with. And don't you know it, this big guy starts calling me out. I hear, "hey pretty boy! Hey pretty boy with the long silky hair! You for me! You gonna be mine." The new inmates were told that we couldn't talk or respond to anyone or anything during "the walk". One thing about doing time is you can't ever bitch out. Once you show the slightest weakness, you lose. Put your balls on your sleeve and make sure everyone knows you will fight. I turned to the inmate next to me and asked, "Is he talking to me?" The guy says, "you're the only one over here with long hair aint ya?" I dropped my things. I looked around to assess the situation. The guy was about 5'10", 200lbs. He was about 20 yards from me; the guards were 50 feet away. Fuck it! I took off running at him full speed. I yelled "fuck you mother fucker, you gonna be my bitch!" He got himself set to handle all the fight I had in me but before I made it to him I was T-bone tackled by a guard I didn't see coming! Holy wow did that fucking hurt. The wind was knocked out of me. I couldn't breathe. The guard was on top of me wrestling me around. I was trying to gasp but couldn't, then I tasted gasoline in my mouth. Then the burning sensation set in. It wasn't gas. I was being sprayed with mace from a couple different directions. I thought I was dying! To keep from taking any more of the pepper spray to the face I rolled over. The guards proceeded to hog tie my hands to my feet behind my back. I was carried like that to the "block" and thrown on the floor of a shower stall where the guards left me tied while they sprayed me with a huge hose. The entire time I heard voices and yelling. I couldn't comprehend much of anything. What I do know is I didn't back down. I went after him. I spent my first official six days of this stretch in "the hole" for attempting to fight and insubordination. That's what the guards put on the report. I was simply making a name for myself. And get this, when I finally did make it to my cell; guess with whom they paired me with? That's right, the guy who called me out in the first place! Bobby.

Bobby was a triple lifer. He'd been there 26 years before he'd seen my face. As I approached the bunks I saw him sitting at a table and I had to pass right by him. I made eye contact and he realized who I was. I just stopped. I kind of nodded my head like it was on again. I dropped my things again. I said, "Ready"? He stopped me real quick by saying, "Settle down there little daddy. I aint got nothing for you. You in a honor dorm. No shit goes down in here, inmate rules." I said, "So what now? I gotta be looking over my shoulder for you?" He explained a few things real quick and said not to worry about him. He says, "You know how it is being down man, I'll never see the free world again. I gotsta get what I can, ya dig?" I kind of laughed with him but I never let my guard down.

Three weeks after I was sentenced, one of the members of my band (the bassist) wrote me and informed me all about the sex Tammy was having with him and the drummer both before and after we got married. Five weeks into the sentence, I got the divorce papers from her. I learned the hard way that she'd emptied my bank account. I had less than eight thousand to help me survive in prison for the next five years.

This prison was called "The Farm". There were 300 acres of fields that were tended by the inmates. We grew everything they wanted. It was okra, corn, potatoes, tomatoes etc. Most of what was produced was sent to the prison kitchens to feed the inmates but there were a few things that were sold at the local markets. Hay is one of them. You ever had to bale hay? That right there is the hardest work I've ever had to do. We had to run up to a bale of hay that was cut and bundled in these large fields, usually they are about 60-80 pounds, we had pick them up and throw it on a moving truck pulling a flatbed trailer. After you release it, we had to run up to the next available bale and do it again. I was completely exhausted after for fourth or fifth one. But you can't stop. If you do you get a write-up for some stupid charge. If you get a write-up, you get sent to the block. If you get sent to the block, you have to face what is called "the kangaroo court". It's just a panel of guards handing out extra duty work detail for your offense. If you get extra duty you have to work the farm on the weekend. And that sucked! I never understood that. Make someone do more of what they've already shown you they can't do. But this is prison after all, Ninety-nine percent of these guys deserved to be here. I saw the guards pull this stuff on old guys that would pass out from heat exhaustion! The worst was this one guy who was about sixty-five years old, he was vomiting and being carried off the field by two other inmates, he had no control of his body at this point; I mean snot and blood was pouring from his nose and everything! The highest ranking guard on the scene had him sent to the block for refusing to work. I was just another number that better "get my cut", meaning I had to handle the work load I was given. But I found myself doing the extra duty a couple times.

I was working extra duty in the rain one time. I had to pick up cigarette butts from the rec yard for twelve hours straight. This guard had a group of us out there. I was just doing what I was supposed to be doing when the guard called me over to him. He was finishing smoking a cigarette and says to me, "You missed one." then dropped the one he had to his feet. I held back everything in my head. I never let my face give the slightest notion of a thought. I just stepped forward, bent over and reached to pick it up. The guard turned around real quick as I bent down and he farted literally right in my face. With my emotions kept in stone I said nothing, I did nothing. He on the other hand thought it was the funniest thing he'd ever done. I simply put the butt in my bucket, took the pain and began looking for more. It's the most degrading moment I've ever known.

Thirty months into my stretch, I was half-way through my sentence and was up for an early parole hearing. I was granted it! No-one ever makes an early parole. I think I sold the parole board on the fact that I was driven to make it in show business. They asked me about my occupation almost immediately. I said that I'm a stand-up comedian and sidekick hack vocalist for a heavy metal rap band. One board member said," Well that explains what it says here. It says Occupation; Amusement and Recreational Service". It seemed the whole board got a kick out of hearing me speak about my goals. I suppose they were used to the answers being dead end jobs like car washes and trades.

I was granted parole by the state parole board. You would figure they would be doing the calling of parole officers and all that. Some sort of communication to alert the proper people of this grant. After all, this was a very rare grant. But they did nothing of the sort. I don't think anyone knew what to do and put my file somewhere.

My release date arrived. My dad drove about nine hundred miles to pick me up and they wouldn't release me, even though I had court documents proving I was to be released on that date. The parole office in that state knew nothing of my release. The prison officials knew nothing. They saw my papers, "Yep those are true legal documents, but we can't let you out". And they didn't, but they did allow my father an extended visit with me.

I was anxious. I was supposed to be going home but I wasn't. I didn't fret it too much at the moment because I knew that it was just another small matter of time to get the paperwork straight, and bam be done. I can do another few weeks. I had no choice. I had to! I was just sorry that my dad had driven all that way for nothing. I hadn't seen anyone, friends or family for three years. I never wanted my dad to see me as an inmate, but I wasn't going to deny him or myself this visit. I walked into the visitation room expecting it to be a contact visit; meaning we could sit in the same room at a table with the ability to at least give each other a hug, but it wasn't. It was the standard glass wall and phone booth visit. I remember looking over the booth dividers searching for my dad as I walked the length of the room. I remember this walk well. The memory always seems to be in slow motion. Each step I took was filled with more anticipation then then last. I looked in each window as I past them. I found him! There he was. We made eye contact. He had a look of unsureness. He was bewildered I think. He didn't say anything when I reached him. He just looked at me. I made the initiative to sit a pick up the phone. "Hey Man," I said. "I'm sorry you drove all the way here for this." He said "Son, for the first time in your life I see you as a man. I wasn't sure if I ever would. But I just did. Seeing you was worth the trip. And I'll be back when your release date is official."

We spent an hour or so catching up. He told me what was going on with everyone back home and I told him prison stories. And that was that. My dad drove home alone and I went back to my cell.

As it turned out I had to be the one to contact the parole office, from prison, from three states away to handle this. Two weeks later, still waiting for clearance, I got in a fight with a guy. When I last saw him, he was alive. He punched me in the back of the head over some stupid occurrence in the chow hall. I just kicked the shit out of him, knocked him out and left. When the guards found him, he was dead. No I did not kill him. Another inmate who had a different beef with him did. He was charged and convicted. I was stripped of my good time for the fight and now doing five years flat. Now ain't that a bitch? Some people call it Karma.

I just did what I had to do. I figured all the wrong I did as a kid was all catching up to me. All the stealing and bullshit I put my folks through... This is was the real punishment. "Cest La Vie." I told myself. Followed by a "What comes around goes around." And for me, my favorite line, "Take the pain".

I kept my mouth shut and eyes open. I'd made a few friends in prison this time. Getting to trust someone is real hard after going through my ordeal, but I did find one. After talking his ear off in the first six months we served together he said the infamous words, "You should write a book." So I gave it a shot. I made a weak attempt to tell the tales from my life. I titled it, "Loves Prey". It seemed though the book was a long ass complaints letter more than a story of trials and tribulations. But who was I to judge. I had written stories and poems and songs my whole life but had no credentials. I figured maybe someday I would publish something. Why not this? But after reading it, I was disappointed. It sounded good when I was writing it. But not when I read it. So I just put it away to save.

I ended up spending a total of seven and a half years behind those bars. I did as much as I could to reflect and rehabilitate myself through writing and studying. I went through a class and received a GED just to see if I could get one. I wrote song after song and sent them to the band I was working with. They usually were pretty close to what I had in my head with what they produced. I wrote another book called "No Jailhouse Bull". The two books I wrote while there will never be published. It seems that all the handwritten work I had in my footlocker was a fire hazard. Inmates aren't allowed to have 16,000 pages of writing in their possession. The guards burned them in a metal drum outside the prison barracks. They were laughing and messing with me saying things like, "See, I told you these were fire hazards, look at all them pages burn!" I was frozen. I just watched, and took the pain.

Anyway, in the final months of my sentence I joined the Toastmasters, a writing and speech club. Ever heard of Toastmasters? I was one of them. The officer in charge of this club was also a police officer in the local community. He didn't have any extra special likening for me but after I'd spent a few months as an active member of the club he pulled me aside. He said he liked my abilities in giving speeches. He'd heard me time and time again telling my tales in the meetings. As it turns out he was also an active member of the "D.A.R.E." program. Every year this program would invite a select inmate to tell his tales to the local schools. I was perfect for this. With my background, are you kidding me? I jumped all over it. I had a few weeks to work on my speech and have it approved. I was told to keep it under twenty minutes and in no way could I use profanity or any "criminal scare tactics". If I could do that then I would be the inmate invited. There were several inmates that were qualified for the job. One inmate had done the speech before, but I was the only toastmaster. So I wrote my speech and I practiced it several times with the club. Now came the time for the D.A.R.E. program to choose which inmate they wanted to go to the schools with them. They had us give our speeches to groups of "bad kids" brought in to the prison. These tours were to show the kids where they were heading. A few of the guards that knew me wanted to see how I'd do. It was surreal in a way that I can't describe. I can only tell you what happened. These guards I speak of adjusted their work schedule so they could attend. They knew my story of how I took the rap for my ex-wife and friend. We talked a lot, me and these guards. When the toastmasters club would meet, they were the guards that escorted the inmates to the club room. They had heard me speak a lot. They knew I was funny. I always had a sense of humor with my speaking in the group. Generally they liked me but couldn't ever say they wanted to be my friend. Although they all said, "If we had met under different circumstances it would be hard not to be".

My first time to speak to a group of kids was coming up and I was nervous! I hadn't had my stomach wheeze from nerves like that in a long time. As I did the speech I felt like I was performing again. It felt good. I had the right message. Basically it was from the reality perspective. I lived in jail. The choice was mine. We are faced with decisions every day, right or wrong is your choice. This is where the wrong choices bring you.

My timed finished was nineteen minutes and twelve seconds. Then there was an unexpected question and answer period. I answered two questions as best I could without sounding like an idiot or criminal. I stepped off of the one-step stage towards the guards who brought me and heard a few claps from the kids for my speech. I looked up. Then the room joined in. I only took about four steps and I reached the guards. The one, who was holding the waist and wrist cuffs, was smiling and saying "Nice job" and also giving a little applaud. I remember watching the chains wiggle around as he motioned his hands like he was clapping. How odd? But it still felt really good.

And so I did receive the invite. As much as I'd like to say that I really did that good, I can't. I mean, yes I did well but I knew there was more to it. I wasn't in on a violent crime. It was a drug charge. Hence, D.A.R.E. this was about drug awareness for kids. The other inmates were hardened criminals. I was the least risk. And I'm glad I was. I did my speech for seven schools, three middle schools and four high schools. The last one I did was videotaped by a local probation office. I had one chance to watch it but was told I couldn't have a copy. But there was a surprise for me that day. It was held out until the close of that speech. It was a guest appearance by the arresting detective in my case!

I finished my speech and before I walked to the side of the stage to get all chained up, in front of six hundred students in a high school auditorium, the detective who arrested me walked up to the podium, told me to stay there for a second, and grabbed the microphone. He spoke for several minutes about things he'd seen being a cop. He mentioned some criminals he's faced. But he said he'd never met anyone like me. He told them the story of our conversation in his car that night. He used words like intelligent, artistic, integrity in his opinion of me. He also used "stupid" but everyone caught the joke. He said how he kept an eye on me throughout my sentence and told them I was about to be released. He ended with hopes that each and every one of them would gain something from the experiences I shared with them. He then turned to me and shook my hand. He did the old lean in and whisper in the ear move and said, "Think you could be my friend now?" I smiled and said "Yes, we could be friends."

I thought it would be really cool to become friends with guy who arrested me. There's something I could write about! But three weeks before I was released, the detective died from complications with liver cancer.

Chapter 9

Get out, get on

The date arrived for release, and my dad made the nine hundred mile trip, again. This time I got out. I was given the option of being released at 12:01 am or wait until business hours (8am), like most everyone else I watched walk out those gates, I chose the midnight release. When an inmate is a "short-timer" he becomes a target for trouble. And in a morning release you are venerable to the sick inmates that will try to get you in trouble so you can't leave. All they have to do is walk up to you and start a fight. It doesn't matter if you don't fight back, you still get sent to the block and chance losing good time. It's called a jealousy bath. So being released while everyone is locked in their cages is the wisest choice.

In a small twisted ceremony, it was customary for the inmate being released to receive a bugler cigarette from an inmate doing a life sentence. If he didn't get one it was supposed to mean that he'd return. I did get one. I got it from Bobby, the guy that wanted to punk me out the first time we met. Bobby handed the cigarette folded in a piece of bread. He didn't want anyone knowing he was giving it to me. He said, "I knew you'd make it outta here lil daddy, I don't wanna see you back now, Ima punk you fo sho if you do ya dig?"

I made that final stroll down "the walk". It was a clear night and quiet like I'd never heard the place. I actually listened to my footsteps as I made my way out. I kept my eyes open and soaked in as much as I could from that walk. Making sure I would never forget it, as a reminder to not return.

This prison exit was not like you see in the movies. The walk leads you up to a gate, but the gate didn't open to the street. This gate opened and leads you to an office in the visitor's parking lot. Only one guard walked me out. He unlocked the chain from the gate and it swung open kind of slow. I saw my father standing in the office and I smiled. A guard standing in the office with him unlocked the door and let me in. My dad and I gave each other a hug that I'll never forget. We broke from the embrace almost in tears and he says, "I'm proud of you son. You stood up for something and stuck to your guns. You made it worse for yourself by fucking up in there but what you just did is admirable in my eyes. You ready to get outta here?" What do you think I said? The last thing I saw in there was a count posted on the wall. It said total inmates 10,887. I didn't realize the prison held that many.

As my father carried my bag to his car, I thought real quick to mess with the ol man's head a little. I pulled the gifted cigarette I received from Bobby out of my shirt pocket and placed it behind my ear. Bugler is cheap pouches of tobacco that you roll into cigarettes yourself. As soon as we sat in the car I started looking out all the windows like I was checking for cops. My dad was staring at me not sure of what I was doing. I grabbed the bugler and kept it cupped in my open hand. I started to hand it over and I said, "Here, fire that bad mother fucker up!"

I thought my dad was going to shit! Real quick I broke it open to show him what it really was. I laughed because it was funny to me, but he didn't think so. I thought of that guard who thought it was so funny to fart in my face. I didn't think it was so funny. I apologized to my father. He pointed to the cigarette and said, "Let's go get you some of the manufactured kind". He cranked up the engine and took me out of there.

My father really surprised me with a gesture / gift that solidified the bond between us as father and son. On the road just out of the parking lot, as we passed by the length of prison walls and razor wire fences, he hands me a cassette tape. It was my band. He got a copy from someone and listened to it on the ride up to get me. It was the album the band released during my "stay". I didn't write or produce any of it. It was all them. My dad says in a light hearted tone, "man that shit sucks! I don't get it! But it sounds as bad as the rest that shit out there so you might have something there! I don't know." It was awesome. My dad took an interest. That's all I kept thinking.

I popped the tape in and for the next 14 hours we talked about a plan for me to get on my feet.

Attention readers, fasten your seat belts, we will be experiencing life at ludacris speed. Right out the gate, I had 24 hours to check in with my parole officer. Then he said I had one week to get a job, and pay this and do that. I didn't realize it until I had been back home but I was on a special parole release. It was called Intrastate Compact Services. I was what they called a "flight risk". This means if an inmate were released to another state he had to have a parole officer in every state connecting them. I had three. So I had three drug screens every month at 30 bucks a pop, three reports to file, and just way too many hours of community service. I had 2 ½ years to complete 500 hours.

48 hours after I got home, the band threw me the "welcome home party." There were a lot of new faces. I walked in, in a haze of precautions. It still felt strange not being locked up. AND THEN BAM! Right off the bat, there she was... perfect. "Hey my best friend's wife... who is the hottie over by the window?" I asked my best friend's wife who was standing next to me. "That's Claudia, Trek's girl; she's off limits." I said "DAMN! He always gets the hot ones!"

After party and catching up time came for me to focus on my life. Here's what was going on in my daily routine.

My last year in prison my baby sister Marie and I were keeping in tight contact, We were making plans for me to live with her until I got on my feet. She was going through a world of shit at the time. She had found herself pregnant at a young age and the father didn't stick around, although before the baby was born, she met another guy who dropped everything in his life to be with her. I mean he didn't miss a beat! He did it all; he married her, adopted the baby, gave her another one, and in the meantime he bought the house and cars too. He was the one who asked me if I needed a place to call home when I got out. And at the time when I got out, He and Marie were about one year in with raising our other sister's Linda's three children. Linda had made wrong choices and life had her registered as one of those addicts that lost. This girl, my sister Linda, Jesus Christ! I'll tell you what, I felt so bad for her. I thought I had problems. She found herself as a lifelong crack addict with her family ripped apart. "Bending over backwards for it", were the exact words she used, and just to keep matters in perspective for me and my problems, Linda was now seven months pregnant with her fourth child. This one came from a guy who raped her while she slept after a six day power binge and he also infected her with HIV. I guess my problems weren't that bad. Linda was about to lose her kids to the state because of her addiction. Marie and her man stepped up to the plate and became legal guardians while she checked into a rehab and straightened out. And she did it! I was released from prison shortly before she did. So my first few weeks of freedom were spent in the usual family chaos that I was so familiar with.

I got to work right away. My brother-in-law hooked me up with a labor job. I had a down payment for a car in three weeks. I went to a friend of my dad's to sell me a descent car for a low, low price. It was nothing shady or illegal. All legit, I took the car and got a nighttime job delivering pizzas. On the days I didn't work the labor job, I worked part time at La-Z-Boy, not in the stores but in the delivery dept. I took this job full time after a year though. It was great money. Three nights a week after my shift at the pizza shop, I would go to the band's warehouse to practice. Oh yes, I was on a mission. I had to give it my all. I couldn't waste anymore time. I was now 30 years old. And look at me. I said to myself "I'm not getting any younger and I'm running out of time." more than once. I had to do everything physically possible to make a run at reaching my goals. So I tightened the grip and kicked life in drive. I handled three jobs, and found time to get a girlfriend. And she had a fifteen year old kid! His name is Ray and hers is Faye. She was actually one of the nicest people I've ever met. Her kid was pretty cool too. We spent the first year together just trying to make heads and tails of what we wanted from our relationship. We were in it pretty serious. We found ourselves living together pretty quick. I even signed the dotted line put her in her favorite little sports car.

Besides working and handling a relationship, I managed the band through three CD releases in the next three years and did 100% of the booking and marketing for our shows. I was also the roadie in charge of handling the equipment on every gig. I would rent a truck if we needed. I was there for every pre-gig load up. I drove the equipment to each gig and I helped with setting up. Then I still had to perform the gig. Then do a tear down and pack of all the equipment from the stage to the truck, only to return to the warehouse to unload and wind up doing it alone because none of the band members came to help. They knew it would get done because they trusted me with their stuff. And was always the same old bull when I asked why didn't they come back to help. "Oh I'm sorry dude, I thought everyone was going back and I just had to get home, or I was in no shape to drive, etc." I never truly felt appreciated for everything I did. I thought that if you lead by example. Your crew will join right in right? I mean, especially since you're working on their futures, right? Not with this bunch.

Nope. Nothing stopped me though. I knew this was what I wanted to do and the only way to do it is to work hard and apply myself. The music we were writing was flat out, great stuff. I believed in its talent. I just knew we had at least one top forty hit that would give us our break. Every dime spent on these three albums came from my pocket. I spent a good thirty grand on the Cd's we'd released. I did get a hundred bucks from the bass player once. I was like, "That's it?" I needed funds to advertise our shows and releases. It killed me that he wouldn't cough up about ten grand. The bass player quadrupled my annual income. I guess he didn't feel as strong about the band's potential.

In addition to paying for all the recordings, truck rentals, and cd releases, I was also covering the drummer's band dues every month for years because he was always broke and never had a job. Band dues are collected from each member so we can have a warehouse to practice. But Craig, the drummer, this guy I'll tell you what, he didn't work. In the four years he was with us he tallied five months of actual employment. Motivation was his enemy. He skated through life preying on the kindness of his friends and family to do everything for him. Of course

I didn't know this until I hired him into the band. What really bothered me the most was something Craig did that affected me personally. Craig didn't know anyone in our circle of friends when he was hired into the band. He got the chance to ask out Claudia, the girl I was interested in at the welcome home party, my friend Trek's girlfriend. Man she was hot. But Trek was my friend and you just don't go after your friend's girl. It ain't right. But at this time Claudia and Trek had split up and she was on the rebound when I hired Craig. One month later she was pregnant with Craig's kid. Five more months, they were married. Damn! That's just typical "me" stuff. I'm never the hero. And I never get the girl. Whatever, It is what it is. Just take the pain as usual.

I was still balls to the wall dead set on making everything happen for the band. I actually set it up to release our album "Bout Time" to coincide with my release from parole. Which, by the way I completed with an impeccable record. So here, I stood on a stage, free from the legal system, no pending charges, a new album being released, everybody saying "don't forget us little people when you make it." I said, "We have to make it first." Let's not get ahead of ourselves.

One of our biggest fans was a guy named Ronnley. He was a cousin to our singer. He spouts off with, "You know I think you really have something here with the new cd. You're almost there." I hated saying what I was about to say because it sounded just like my dad, but I said it because it was true. "Almost don't count." An interesting fact about Ronnley is he was a wealthy man. He made my bass player look like a welfare case. I know he could have come up with some major bank to help us get a little more recognition. I even asked him to thrown down some cash one time. I had a small get together at my house to simple give the band a "cheers" for completing the project and Ronnley attended. He got offended or seemed insulted when I asked him if he believed in us enough to pitch in. I didn't understand. Well after a fifteen minute conversation that got quite heated, Ronnley didn't invest. I believe I said the things to insure he never would. Honestly even if I didn't say those things, I wasn't getting a dime out of him. I understood that. I took the opportunity to unleash some pent up anger. Oh well. Another door closed. NEXT!

The release of the CD went off with every hitch you could possibly imagine! Problem after problem with the band, transportation, equipment, the venue itself, I mean you name it! Not one detail went smoothly. But I made it happen. We sold out of the cd on the first night. The bar we held the release party in logged a record in profit. The owner said we could have full range of the place whenever we wanted. Things were looking good.

The 2:30am Call

To my knowledge there are only three kinds of calls at 2:30 am. They are the; drunk call, the booty call, and a bearer of bad news.

While I spent all efforts at this time in my life on my career and working, like I mentioned earlier, I did find myself in a relationship with Faye. She was about ten years older than me. She was a country girl and like I said, sweet as can be. I got the worst 2:30am call in my life when she and I were together. It was a Sunday night (Monday morning) I almost didn't answer it but I had made a promise to the band members if they were ever too drunk to drive, to call me since I don't drink. I would pick them up to take them home. I felt they were my investment and this was a way to show my dedication as a member. I had kept my promise about seven or eight times already when this call rang. I answered it expecting to hear, "I'm drunk dude". Instead I hear a woman's voice "Yes sir, Are you the brother of Linda Lucas?" I answer yes. I don't remember what exactly what she said but it was something like, "I'm sorry to bother you at this hour but I'm a sheriff's deputy here in town and I have bad news for you. I'm here with Linda's children. I need you to come get them because your sister is deceased. She overdosed on heroin."

Of course I jumped up and started ranting to Faye. There wasn't much to think about. I was out the door and on my way. Faye was right there with me!

It was only about seven minutes from the time the call came in until I arrived to the scene and what I saw, I didn't expect. It was crazy! My sister wasn't dead after all! The paramedics gave her the adrenaline shot to her heart. Twice! I got out of the car expecting to see a body bag instead I saw my sister fighting three or four paramedics that were trying to strap her to a gurney. I was almost catatonic. I was in disbelief. Faye jumped out of the car and ran up to the officer that was with the children. The kids watched the whole thing. In shock, and nervous the kids came with home with us. We had a lot of things changing in our lives. I certainly hadn't a clue of what to do. I just knew like I'd always known, no matter what, family sticks together.

My sister ultimately had taken three adrenaline shots before her body kicked back in and stayed beating.

By nine am I was a zombie. Both Faye and I had called off from work to handle the immediate actions that needed to be taken in a case like this. First off Faye was gung ho for taking in the kids and keeping them with us. I didn't argue. My intentions were to be there for them. My baby sister Marie had already done this and now I had to. Then the state had something to say. My sister Linda had a file with the DCF. (Dept. of children & family) They called me and asked for my address so they could come get the kids to place them in foster care. I was mortified! "No way" I said. I told them that my place was big enough and I had the finances to raise them. Besides "I'm family!" I said. Why wouldn't the state want them to live with family!? She responds with, "Oh we do, but none with your criminal record." (OUCH! Yeah, that hurt.) I gave her the address and twenty minutes later two sheriff patrol cars came racing up to my place like the dukes of hazards! They slammed on their brakes and skidded to a halt in my driveway. The kids stayed in the house and I just calmly walked outside and up the officers and said hello. "You are here to pick up the children I presume?" I then asked, "Where is the DCF representative?" One of the officers said she called them saying I gave her a false address. I said you guys are here; the kids are in the house. Does that seem like a false address? They both told me they found the place real easy. "I just spoke her a few minutes ago! I gave her directions!" I swear! She was a new agent and this was her first case. Go figure. It's just my luck. But alas, what had to be done legally, had to be done. I could not keep the kids with me. I talked with the kids briefly and told them not to worry. I said I will do everything possible to keep them with our family, but right now they must go with these people. That crushes me every time I think of it. It crushed even more so when I had to watch them walk out of my house and get into police cars not knowing what's going to happen next. They were lost and scared. The look on their faces was like I let them down. Guilt swept through me and I felt like crying. There wasn't anything I could do. They all just looked out the windows at me standing in my driveway. Their faces faded to black as they were driven away.

I got a call from my father and his new girlfriend the next day. They were stepping up. They wanted the kids with them. They could adopt the kids from the state but there were miles of red tape to fight through and as well expected, a substantial amount of finances needed to pull this off. My father and his girlfriend Stevie had to be married and out of debt and too many I's to dot and T's to cross. But this ends up like it was supposed to. I had fifteen grand that I'd been saving it up for recording the next cd with the band but this was way more important. I gave my dad half of it. It was enough to cover the bare minimum. My dad came up with money to ease the transition but things were not top notch. They would be living life the same as I remember growing up. The place was a trailer, small and cramped, on an acre or two in a small town. Except the location was in the South not the Midwest.

My dad and Stevie married, I was the best man and they were awarded custody of all three children. The kids were now in a stable home and remained with family. I relaxed once everything was said and done. During the legal battle of all this I remained working my day jobs of delivering furniture & pizza, and detailing cars. I still did everything I could for the band. I only had part of the money I'd saved and couldn't afford to record all of the band's new music; so we released a cd called "Phuque U You Phuqin Phux". It was a five song LP we put out to raise the money to release the full cd masterpiece, "Old Dogs New Tricks." I'll tell you what, if we had all the money like the big shot studios and record labels, we would have been on top. But we didn't. It was just me and what I could scrape up. It was just my dreams, and me. It seemed I was the only one with a dream. I was the only one going after one. These guys went through the motions hoping that we'd get signed by a major record label, but never made any moves to knock on the doors. It was to the point that I had to convince myself I was using these guys for their talents. I didn't feel like we were striving at goals together. Everyone had his or her own objectives. Mine was to be rich and famous. Like always.

It took about a year for me to put together enough cash to record the last cd and it left me broke. I wasn't sure where I was going to end up. At this point Faye and I went our separate ways. The situation with my sister and her kids and my dad adopting them was brutal on our relationship. We split up but remained friends.

So here I was again, single, just me and my dreams. I remained at the place where Faye and I lived but I didn't do so well at keeping up with the bills. I found myself stuck it a rut.

I was two months behind on rent and still paying to finish the cd release. Believing in the band's talent, I continued on. I heard a saying once that I was trying to follow. "If you want something, you have to risk something. If you want something bad enough, you risk it all." And of course, I did. And I failed.

As great as I felt the band's last recording sounded, not one person or record label showed interest in backing us. Wait, yes, there was one. This one guy did. I went to drop off some cd copies to sell on consignment at a local music shop. The owner, Lester, a self-proclaimed "huge fan" (but we never saw him at any shows) drops the cd in his player and cranks it up. He acted like he was going to show everybody he could. There was a guy there listening to it with us. He bought the first copy. The man asked what I did for the band. I spun the tale real quick in the fast talking banter for which I am widely known, throwing in the jokes when plausible and right on time. Never giving anyone a chance to respond before I'd hit another zinger. The guy was well dressed and spoke highly of what he was hearing from us. He said he was involved with a huge historic band and would be happy to show them this. I was like "AWESOME" man, please do, and feel free". He asked if we were playing anywhere and I was all over it telling him that we were releasing the album that night! I worked out the release of this CD with opening for another 1980's hair band's old singer. The gentleman laughed at who it was, but was impressed more that we were at least on a national circuit. Making sure I knocked on every door, I didn't hesitate to throw the guy a few tickets to the show that night. I probably took it a bit overboard, (like I have so many times) and autographed the cd he bought.

That night, at the release party, the gentleman from the music store showed up, in a Lamborghini Diablo. He said it wasn't his; he had borrowed it from the singer in the band he worked for. You would think at this time, if this guy likes me OH MY GOD! I'm in. If I played my cards right, I would achieve the goals I dreamed about since I lived in the trailer when I was six years old. My spirits were high; another opportunity was placed before me.

With a flawless approach to our lead in song, the band's music had blended in with a slow rising level as the crowd noise subsided. The venue was practically filled to capacity. The song we opened with has a thunderous slam of instruments called a "crunch" that draws your immediate attention. We hit it! "CRUNCH"…You pause and hold your breath. You wait for the next "CRUNCH" so you can slash your hands through the air in perfect timing with them. The song kicks in and the band plays on. The crowd is banging their heads in unison. The whole place was energized!

I was not on stage yet. I was doing something at the sound board; I think I was adjusting some lights. After the first song, I made eye contact with the guy who'd come to see us. He gave me one of those looks like he'd just seen a hot chick. He mouthed," they're good, I'm going to like this." And with a big smile he took a drink of his beer.

The second song began, again, another high energy track that keeps your heart pumping. We were shocking this man. He was jamming. He began yelling and screaming in applause! By the time we started the third song

I'm telling you, the band was on fucking fire. The timing was running perfect. The sound tech knew his shit as well. It was so good that one of our fans got a bit overzealous in the mosh pit. Well there wasn't a mosh pit, the club didn't allow them, but our fan wanted one! The bouncers warned him a few times to stop but to no avail, he didn't and they threw him out. Then my band, the band that I did everything for, said, "let him back in or we are not playing"' I ran on stage and told them, "Fuck that guy! If you don't play I don't get paid!" I did all the work for this show. The lead singer said, "If they aint letting him back in, I aint playing." He unplugged the keyboards and the microphone then walked off stage. The whole band followed suit. Fifteen minutes later after we had a mad scramble of tearing down all the equipment so the headline act could set up. I was standing in the front of the club when the visiting gentleman walked out. He said that was the best band that will never make it. "They're great! But, sorry, you can't do these things and expect anyone to talk seriously do you? Good luck."

What did I learn here? Stay out of trouble, work hard, be true, follow your dreams, chase your dreams, work harder, set it up and watch everybody you are doing it all for destroy it. I took it with a grain of salt, along with the pain.

Chapter 10

Mystery Blessing

I just kept plugging away. I came up with another concept to get the band back in the studio for another cd recording; I still worked my jobs while managing the band. I never stopped trying. I was broke after that last failure. I paid what bills I could but found myself in a desperate situation. This time it wasn't drugs or prison. It was just life. My pride kept me from asking anyone for a loan. Everyone I knew had their own financial woes. Then someone unexpected gave me a hand. It turned my altered my life.

I had a few high dollar auto detailing accounts that I tended to on Sunday's. I did them every Sunday for five years. I was like clockwork. And I did excellent work. The cars were awesome, an F355 spider Ferrari, a couple BMW's, a few Benz', a 63' & 74' corvette, a couple boats and a plane! I made an average of $300 before noon every time I showed up. It really helped so I always did good work.

My clients weren't what I expected at all. The first time I showed up to meet them I got nervous turning into their house. The driveway leads to a four million dollar home. It was absolutely beautiful. It's exactly like how I've always wanted to live. The people knew from my demeanor that I was basically from the street, not of their class so to speak. But they were great. They talked to me like I was a friend. I didn't feel like "the help". They were down to earth, very funny, cultured, kind and witty. I really enjoyed doing the work for them. They got to know me real well and turned me on to some friends of theirs that also wanted a personal auto detailer. One friend's name was G.P.

I was waxing G.P.'s boat one glorious Sunday morning when he walked out his dock as he did some times to chat with me. We had a bunch of conversations over the year that I'd been working for him. We started chatting about the stuff we always wound up talking about, cars and women and life. He liked me because he himself came from the same background as I. He knew all about my trials and tribulations and I knew his. He was cool. He gave advice all the time when I'd tell him stories from the band and home life. Well apparently he felt how bad I was struggling and helped me out. He asked me if I would let him help me. He offered me $1,000.00. He said he would never do this for just anyone. He trusted I would do the right thing. He saw the drive in me to succeed. He even liked my band's music, a little. He offered this money on the pretenses that I would work off the debt. He didn't want me to feel as if I was accepting a hand out. He sensed my pride from the start. I also had to promise that it would not be spent on the band. I did so and accepted.

The Friday morning prior to this Sunday I woke up looking around my place for change so that I could get a cup of coffee on my way to work. I found a dime, a nickel, and four pennies. "It's gonna be a rough weekend" I said. Although I was getting paid on this day from both my furniture delivery job and the pizza delivery job, I would still be $850.00 short of what I owed. This was it. By Monday I was going to be living in my car. I don't know if Karma took care of me, God, or Allah, or whoever! But this is what happened. I needed $1,700.00. My furniture check was $675, pizza check was $167, in addition to that I made $130 in tips for Friday & Saturday, I made the usual $300 for detailing on Sunday, and now I had $1,000 advance from the most unlikely source. All of it paid off my debt and left me $500 in the black. I was back in black! And I never looked back. I was making enough money to handle my bills I had just spent too much on the band and not delegated my finances well. This gesture saved me.

I worked off the advance in no time and looked forward once again to accomplishing my goals with the band.

Thank you G.P. You helped me more than anyone ever had. I'll never forget your trust.

Chapter 11

Back on track, well kinda

The last album the band and I did was the end all to be all, of my whole existence; this was the something that I am proud to say "Hear that? That was me". This was the piece that would help me not regret my decision to go this route. I spent more money on this release than all of the others combined. I worked harder at holding the band together as we worked things along. We had more of the high school mentality arguments. The drummer Craig had his problem with the guitarist Pat over a debt that wasn't paid. Craig was being a dick. His actions spoke volumes about his mental state. He always had an apology after outbursts. He treated his wife Claudia and his child the same way too. I spoke with Claudia about his actions. She swore me to secrecy, and then told me he was seeking treatments for Bi-polar symptoms and Borderline Personality Disorder. I was like "that explains a lot". But we all tolerated it. I needed him to play the drums in the band. The band is what's going to make me rich. I just tried to stay focused. By the time the cd was ready, Craig had pissed everyone off so bad it was crazy.

I managed to set up the CD's release show at the club I wanted. The production of the CD was first rate. The right crowd was there. The owner of the club looking around, happy to see his club filled with patrons, impressed by the turnout. He knew how bad we, as a band, had been treated in other clubs. Another club owner was at this gig and wanted to make things right between us by asking us to open for an extremely popular underground band. I couldn't accept because it conflicted with a pre-existing gig. I had six months invested in that one gig alone. So the offer was declined. It didn't matter anyway because as soon as the show was over, we got the last piece of equipment loaded into the truck, Craig said, "fuck you guys, I quit." I couldn't believe it. He just quit. Everything I just went through and dealt with to make it happen and he just quits! I was so livid I quit too. And then the bass player says," If he quits, that's it, I'm done too". And that was it. The dream chasing ended. I drove the equipment to the warehouse and unloaded everything by myself, one last time.

A few weeks after the band split up I was invited over to the Craig and Claudia's house for a little barbeque. Craig seemed to be in good spirits. I was asked by a longtime friend who was there what my plans were since the band split up. I made a comment/joke about perusing a talk show host position. The next joke was something about censorship and rules and how I wouldn't have a chance of getting on TV. Claudia then says, "Why don't you broadcast it over the internet?"

(Enter the next new dream chasing project here.)

This stuff is everywhere on the internet now, but at the time of this idea, internet shows were in the pioneer stages. There weren't any. We checked. Claudia's step-sister was a paralegal for a popular law firm and handled our legal end; she did research and filed the papers when we bought the domain name. We had to create a company and she did all the leg work on that. It's was called "Netvision Networks Inc." We elected Claudia as the president, because she called it! Actually it was her suggestion. I took the executive producer position as well as the ON AIR personality, because it's my concept and

Craig was, well, nothing! I think we said he could be an on air talent too. He was going to answer questions live from the emails.

Attending this barbeque were a few interesting people. They were Claudia's friends. They were marketing and program directors from the USA and Comedy Central networks. They raised an eye to the idea being shouted back and forth. The next thing you know I was back running around with a pad of paper, writing everything down that comes to mind. This project was all I could think about. I had new fresh blood for this. I could write and come up with the ideas for shows but I had zero knowledge of computer and technical aspects. I left the entire web designing and creating to those interested in the field, which was everybody else! This was awesome. I was working on chasing my dreams with others who contributed equal efforts. And I didn't have to lug any music equipment around!

After we had everything legal with getting the company incorporated, I remained concentrating on show material and ideas. But don't you know it... something always happens to slow you down. Craig started freaking again. This time it was at his home. He went off on Claudia in front of me and I had to leave. He wasn't violent or threatening, but he was just mean. If you remember, Claudia is the girl from my homecoming party that was dating my friend Trek. When Claudia and Trek split up Craig moved in before I could ask her out.

On the night Craig showed his true colors, he got a bit too wordy with Claudia for my taste. He started name calling and degrading like I'd never heard guy. I jumped up and got in his face. I was seconds away from beating him to a pulp. Claudia didn't want that. She and a neighbor stopped me as soon as they saw my mannerisms change. Craig stood there doing nothing. He didn't say a word. I said a few choice words about he should try saying those things to me. He was scared and didn't say a word. He wouldn't even look me in the eye. He was 6'1", I'm 5'6" and he wouldn't budge. He knew what I was capable of doing. Claudia was scared as well. As much as she felt he deserved what I could to him, she did not want to witness this fight. So she stopped me. She was satisfied that someone put him in his place. Never would anyone believe Craig was like this. Now Claudia had witnesses.

It wasn't long after that incident when Claudia told me that she was divorcing him. I told them both I wouldn't be coming around until the smoke clears. And that was that. I went into a shell. I clammed up. We cancelled our Netvision Network idea and I didn't quit my day or night jobs. I remained working to pay my bills. I did switched jobs a few times after the band split up though. I was thinking that I would end up in a business suit like my dad wanted but on second thought... naaaaahhh! I grabbed another delivery job that paid horrible. This one supplied kitchen and bathroom cabinet makers with special plywood's, Formica and hardware. Judging from the interview I had, the branch manager Bill said he had a feeling I would do well working here. He was correct. I did so well that soon after I started the job, Bill fired the warehouse manager and gave me the position. I did so well at that positon, not even a year later; the vice present of the company fired Bill and made me the operations manager! Shortly after Bill was fired, he died. I thought "is it me, do I jinx people?" From the arresting officer I befriended, to this guy Bill, I had my reasons to question!

About a year later I was doing my thing, not doing any sort of creative entertainment, simply working my ass off doing everything

I could to help keep the branch open in the company for which I worked. When on a clear day, Claudia contacted me. This was the era where chatrooms were the craze. Claudia and I hadn't spoken in a while. On this day, she saw me in a chatroom and pops in with, "So you think I'm hot do ya?" I said, "Who told you?" Craig told her one time when he was freaking out. And she remembered it. I took the opportunity right there and told her how much I've adored her and for how long. I didn't care that she was still married to Craig or that they have a child. I was a part of that kid's life before he was ever a thought. I was not going to miss this chance. The next thing she told me was that she had filed the divorce papers from Craig and it would soon be final.

I let her have it. I told her everything. She didn't shy away from the stories of how I used to catch myself admiring her at parties and social gatherings. She was flattered by most of it. And I was in disbelief that I was talking to her about it! Well this reunion got us motivated in getting things going again with our Netvision concept. Of course, one thing led to another and we were a couple. Believe me I forced the issue, I wanted it to happen, I made it happen, she couldn't resist anyways. And I was right. She was the one.

She drove me nuts. I felt ten times more love for this girl than I've felt for all of the loves in my life. You think going to prison to protect my wife was something. I will die for Claudia.

So there it is, a time to remember when I got exactly what I wanted. I got the girl.

We kept our status a secret for a while. I like to believe that Karma had figured that I'd paid enough dues, and this was my change. I was newly inspired, like the first time in my life. She woke the sleeping poet that was a part of me that I knew was there but had never been affected. We wrote letters and poems and sometimes sonnets back and forth. We were on the same page from the start. We filled each other's inbox's with everything we'd made connections on. Ha! Love, it was the best secret I ever had. Once we came out with it, we faced battles. We had all the reality problems, close to what you've seen on any given Jerry Springer show. We both wanted to move away. We could have left anytime to build our lives elsewhere but Craig, loser that he is, yes he was no longer my friend, had a legal tie to his child. Claudia had full custody but he got kid every other weekend.

We had a few bad exchange episodes where I was ready to beat him up because his chaperoning skills were pretty bad. Craig thought it was funny allowing the kid to eat a super king sized candy bar and drinking a soda before bringing him home at 9 pm. on Sunday nights. The sugar rush vomit spells were brutal on the kid's body. After being trained in martial arts for eleven years for the wrong reasons, after being in more than a hundred fights in the state prison, I was ready to destroy this imbecile with my bare hands. I had to keep reminding myself it that I will definitely go back to jail for beating him. What good would I be in jail? I guess those seven and a half years did something. I didn't touch him. Again, I'm not sure if karma plays in here but I hadn't been doing anything illegal. I worked hard, I wronged no one nor did I seek vengeance on my ex-wife and Dr. Vern for what they did to me. And now here, I didn't touch this guy. We actually had the child exchange to be held mandatory at a police station to keep me from doing anything. It worked.

Everything I'd been doing seemed to be paying off. I had a new project to replace the band and I'm sharing that dream with the girl of my dreams. Everything I wanted in a woman, I found in this one.

We took things rather slow with a lot of things that people normally do fast when they fall in love. We wanted to speed things up every day because of the way we felt but we also wanted to be sure we weren't kidding ourselves. We lived our days as if we were a married couple but we slept in separated houses. We had to do a lot of travel and schedule adjusting to make time to see each other. We lived 22 miles apart. Our jobs were 36 miles apart but we found ways to see each other every day. We did that for a year which seemed like week. And then I moved in with her and the child.

Time went by. We grew and grew as a unit. We share an unconditional bonding, it felt like the bond I have with my family. We clicked on all cylinders and every other little saying that expresses that things are good. We set goals together and achieved them. The entire relationship was filled so much love and laughter. The only bad parts were dealing with Craig when it came to their son. Of course we had a ton of arguments about all the other stuff that people have. But we did what we were supposed to do and worked through them. Being honest, most of our fights were because of my reactions to a lot of things I'd never known before. Claudia comes from a tight nit small family. I have more cousins on my mother's side than both sides of her entire family! Claudia is an only child. My difficulties understanding her outlook on family issues caused so many arguments. We disagreed on a constant basis. I grew up poor and starved. I was raised disciplined but not guided. I never wanted a family because of it. The responsibility is overwhelming. Knowing what I did as a child and got away with, I doubted I had what it took to be the "dad" of a family. I wasn't sure if I would beat my kids the way I'd been beaten. I never wanted to be in the situation of disappointing a child with not providing a good Christmas or real food, and new clothes for school so that they wouldn't have to deal with the embarrassment like I did. Could I teach a child right from wrong, good from bad? This is not a stage where I'm acting out a script or giving a speech. I had trouble with the good and bad decisions on my own! At this point in my life all I'd truly ever done was strive to make it in the entertainment industry and work to pay the bills. I'd been up and down the road of drug addiction. I'd been in and out of prison a few times as well! Now here I was, knowing I was in for the long haul. Helping the woman I knew I wanted to spend the rest of my life with, raise her child. Being an only child, Claudia didn't understand from where it is I came. She is no idiot but I was doing and saying things that she'd never saw nor heard. I offended her with a few actions but redeemed myself after learning her perceptions. Living, loving, laughing, learning through this relationship was all new. It was awesome. I loved it. She loved it! We loved it! I loved it so much I said the words I never in a millions years thought I'd say, "Let's have a baby". WHOA! WHAT? I couldn't believe it! I kind of shook my head a little when I said it. But I said it and I meant it.

I took a look around our lives before I mentioned wanting to create a life and saw that my girl and I both had career jobs, both with good pay and benefits, a nice stable place, it was small but nice, it was in a great location for everything. Why not? I argued that her child needed a sibling. I said, "You don't want him growing up like you do you!" She laughed, but she also had a glow in her smile that told me she wanted to have a child too, for all the reasons, all the right reasons.

Even though I never wanted a family of my own, I did have an idea of what the "perfect" family would be for me. It was just four members, Mom, Dad, Son, and Daughter. And the boy is older than the girl. I didn't realize it until the moment my Claudia said "yes, let's have a baby." that I had a 50/50 chance of having that exact family. So when she asked me what I wanted to have I shouted, "A girl! With brown eyes!" She said she wanted another boy. We were both really ok with whichever we were granted but we had our reasons for wanting what we did.

I couldn't believe it still. Here I was now at age thirty-five, planning parenthood! As scared as I was I never once felt challenged. I wanted this with my heart. And so we did. We had a baby. I was practically giddy because even though I have other children out there, here is one that I could watch grow in a belly then come into the world knowing that I would be daddy. It's the most incredible feeling I've ever felt.

I got what I wanted again. We had a girl, with brown eyes!

Chapter 12

Happy Got Me

Without realizing it, my drive to become rich and famous had died. I will always be a driven person. It's just my goals had been replaced with details of taking care of all I could for my family. What I once thought was overwhelming was actually quite easy. It's easy if you're not busy with anything else and you possess the energy that I possess! I no longer had three jobs or had to save anything for a cd recording or warehouse fees for the band. I used to spend hundreds of hours at the studio editing recordings, making calls, booking shows, contracting recording sessions and actual practicing with the band. I had all that time on my hands. I didn't do stand-up any more. I was always going to be in town. All I had to do was make money and be myself with my family.

I doubted myself in whether or not I had what it took to raise children. I found out I did. That fact that Craig was acting like a complete maniac was a true test of how much I had to keep it together. I was now a role model dad to his child. If the child saw me acting like his dad the message of how he should be is distorted. I didn't want him thinking that all men act like that. Well now, was I maturing? Becoming a responsible adult? I sure was.

Claudia and I grew more as a unit in those first years together than anyone I've ever known or heard of for that matter! We managed to pay off eighteen thousand dollars in credit card bills and buy new cars for each other. We were sitting down each night at the dinner table as a family. We held parties and birthdays and gatherings. We went on get-a-ways and vacations. We went to the movies once or twice a month. There were no disappointing moments on Christmas. This is what I wanted for my family when I was a kid. We were doing it. We were providing everything I didn't have growing up! I enjoyed the feeling. Claudia didn't know exactly what that meant to me. This was normal for her. It meant everything to me.

A Tragedy Prefaced Fate and Destiny

If there was ever any good from someone's death this sure is the case, except for the deceased of course, and his immediate loved ones.

Craig, who is now my girlfriend's ex-husband, who is my ex-band's ex-drummer, and the father of the boy I am raising, decides in his ultimate wisdom, to jump on his motorcycle during a tropical storm and ride around town. He had one of those "crotch rockets". I don't know what you know about tropical storms but the winds are in excess of sixty mph with gusts that reach ninety mph. Rain and hail usually accommodate. Who in their right mind would ride a bike through it? Well Craig did. I may be a bit callus by saying he had a date with death and was on time.

Craig's father Harland called Claudia during this tropical storm. I was standing right next to her when the call came in. She knew who it was before she answered by the caller ID feature and thought that maybe he was checking in to see if she and the boy were ok. But he was the bearer of the bad news.

Craig, the drummer, the father, a son, our "ex" was in an accident. A subcontractor for a major phone company, who was out repairing downed phone lines during the storm, was driving his personal work van and ran a stop sign. Craig was speeding down the residential street where the contractor was working. Craig never saw the truck. The guy in the truck never saw Craig. Craig never touched his breaks and hit the back of this van at seventy-five mph. He was dead before his body hit the ground.

Talk about mixed emotions! I went in both directions and didn't know how to handle it. I mean with everything that Craig put us through I wanted to kill him myself, but I didn't want him dead. Does that make any sense? I mean I'd thought about it before, like if he were to die. We wouldn't have to deal with all the childish antics anymore! Things like, he would come by the house in the middle of the night and dump garbage all over the yard. One time I had just completed fixing the front yard with new dirt and sod. He ran a car through it and tore it up. All that shit would stop. We would be freed from the legal bond and could move away. We couldn't afford to buy a house in the location we were in. We were forced to stay there and rent this small house and survive hurricanes and tourist seasons. And it was hot and humid year round. I just took the pain; Claudia and the kid took the pain right along with me. We endured this stuff without response. But now the reality was that it was all over. Craig was really dead. We could do what we wanted now. And so we did.

The sad truth of this is the repercussions with the boy. The boy would never know his true father. I was the male role model he would grow up with. Claudia was torn to shreds over this. She didn't want Craig to die either. She wanted things to be civil. She mourned for her son having to deal with the death of his father. She was young and had to be there as her own father lost his battle to cancer. She remembered the pain and certainly never wanted her son to experience it. Nevertheless, it happened. And all the pain that comes with it was endured.

The positives of this tragedy outweighed the negatives by tenfold from my perspective. Claudia and I at this point had already cleared all debts and saved a little nest egg. I was the boss at my job and she'd been working her way up the ladder at hers. The kids were healthy and happy. We weren't held to a court bond. Time had come to fulfill our destiny.

I spent the better part of ten months at work that year looking on line for a ring to place on Claudia's hand. She had printed a black and white photocopy of one she liked from a website and said this was the ring of all rings. Very nonchalantly I took the print to work and we never spoke of it again. Well I took the picture and forgot what website it came from. I figured I would search a few sites here and there and maybe I'd get lucky and find it. As each week passed and then months, my search for the ring fell short. I wanted to ask her what site it was but I could never find the right scenario in our conversations to bring it up and cleverly retrieve the info without her knowing what I was doing. I couldn't find it. I went so far as to recruit three of my office employees in on the search! They loved helping me. It beat playing solitaire.

Low and behold, I found the ring! Ten months of looking and I found it! It was a big ordeal at work because I told the people helping me search that I would give who ever found it $100.00. They were bummed that no one got the money but were glad the search was over.

I sat back after physically receiving the ring and having a nice stone set in, (and yes, I went to Jared's!) I contemplated on when to propose. The Christmas holidays were approaching so I thought I would just wait until after the New Year. But spontaneity is usually my way to do something you want remembered so I went with that. I didn't plan anything. I would just ask her when the time felt right. That moment happened on Christmas morning.

Christmas morning, after all the gifts were opened, and Claudia was unsuspecting, I pulled the kids aside and gave them the ring to give their mom as we were sitting together on the sofa. I attempted to give instructions. I had to be quick and whisper to them. They were both supposed to ask her to marry me at the same time but we didn't have time to rehearse this stuff. It was a split second decision. It didn't matter though, no matter how unplanned it came off, she was speechless with joy. The quirkiness of the moment made it perfect. She cried, she laughed, and then she said yes.

In what seemed to be a few days, but was actually two and a half years, we were married. We held the ceremony at a Hard Rock Hotel. The kids were the ring bearer and flower girl. My dad was my best man. My friend Pat, the guitarist from the band, sang the song "You belong to me" for the bridal march. It was just perfect. Sammy Hagar even played a cameo role! The wedding ceremony was staged behind the hotel along a landscaped creek and grotto. As we were saying our vows everyone hears Sammy Hagar being pumped through the stage speakers at the hotel pool!

We all started singing "I can't drive 55!" The event coordinator for our wedding went furiously running and calling people to stop it long enough for us to finish!

Our honeymoon was awesome too. Instead of going off somewhere without the kids, we just stayed at the hotel with fifty or so guests for the weekend. We went to all the theme parks adjacent to the hotel. It definitely is at the top of my life's greatest moments.

After all the rollercoasters and rides we could handle, we drove the kids north and out of the state to house shop. Claudia and I were married now and ready to buy a house to raise the kids. We spent a few days looking around an area where my wife's (I can say that now!) employer had their corporate headquarters. She was approved to transfer. I had a friend who owned a fence business in the area. I was able to hammer out a deal for me to manage said business. Everything was falling into place. Although we didn't find a house to buy on that trip, it wasn't long before we found the one we wanted.

And so we found it. Well actually Claudia found it on a website. Her friend Honey lived in the area so Claudia asked her if she would take a look at it. Honey's report was it seemed to be too good to be true. It wasn't though. Honey said "Put your bid in now!" So we did and we got it. (That makes three for me now!)

Here it was, a four bedroom, three full bathrooms, two story split level house with a two car garage on an acre and a half located where the schools are top rated in the nation, close enough to everything, far enough from everyone. It wasn't a "cookie cutter" model. There was no HOA! You might as well live in prison if you live with one of those. We were doing exactly what we wanted to do. We bought a home three times the size of what we were living in and it was a fraction of the prices we'd been seeing. We got away from that humid one-weather state. Our children would learn life with four seasons. That is very cool to me. You're deprived of too much natural beauty without them.

The change in my perspective on life and goals was so grand. My whole life all I wanted to do was make it rich. I wanted to be famous. There wasn't a move I made without that in mind. And here I was, a few years into a life as a family man. I'd spent those years now without thinking of dream chasing. I hadn't screwed up with anything legal. No longer were drugs an influence. It was all replaced with concerns of good schools and making sure the kids are healthy and provided for. And making sure I could continue to woo my wife! They are all that matter to me now.

But of course, not every blessing comes without a hardship.   After the purchase of the home and uprooting the family to another state, my so called friend with the fence business pretty much flat out lied about the position I was going to hold. He actually closed his shop before we made the move and didn't tell me. We bought the house on the pretenses of my employment with him. I had a signed letterhead contract! I could have brought it to court and sued, but why? It wouldn't have mattered anyway. This was during the recession of 2007. No one was calling to have a fence built. He closed the business because of it. Fortunately Claudia's company was a stable firm and she remained with them. We knew we wouldn't be able to keep this place on one income. We also had two car payments and all the other things that were needed to provide life for our family. I just started hammering out resumes and walking the local areas looking for any kind or work. George Bush was in his last year as president and the economy had just fell through the floor when we moved. I couldn't find any work. I filled out hundreds and hundreds of applications on line. To no avail, I remained jobless. A positive from this occurrence was the fact that I was home.

We didn't need to put the baby in a daycare. BING! Score one for the positives! Then I put my mother's lessons to use and started making sure that this four thousand square foot house stayed clean! I scoured and scrubbed every last inch of it. Our son, yes I said our son, was off to school each weekday. Claudia went to work. And I stayed at home with our daughter and became the domestic partner. Claudia and I noticed we hadn't had to take the baby to see a doctor for any illness since we left our previous home which was practically a weekly event for us. The daycare we had our daughter in was dreadfully unclean. It was that and the house we rented. Hurricane Francis in 2004 damaged the roof. Black Mold formed in a section of the attic and went undetected for a year or so but our daughter was always sick. Once we moved to the new house, the sicknesses stopped.

And so day by day, doing what we could to stay above water, the time went by.

The first spring came in the new place and it was time to see what I could do with this big back yard we had. There was a shed that the previous owner had built by himself. He was a horticulturist so he built a greenhouse to it. It was awesome! It had all the timers and drippers and misters and all the bells and whistles that a greenhouse needed. Of course I had to figure it all out with zero knowledge of what I was doing. I started simple. I grew some tomatoes, bell peppers, eggplant and cucumbers.

It was cool. I really enjoyed it. I grew so many tomatoes I didn't know what to do with! I learned to make fried green tomatoes and turned out the family loved them! I talked to my mother and asked for her dad's/my grandfather's recipe to making homemade spaghetti sauce. I was successful in my first attempt. At the time, we were all new to having Facebook accounts. I was taking pictures, posting them, and asking, "Is this how it's supposed to look ma?" And the more stuff I grew in the garden the more things I would post and ask questions about. That first year my dad had made a visit to see us. I had about seventy-five pounds of cucumbers that I couldn't even give away. I grew so many that I had already exhausted everyone I knew with them. My dad suggested that I make pickles. He said he used to make them with his mother when he was a boy. He had some trouble remembering the recipe so we made one up as best we could. They turned out to be awesome. I call them Tickled Pickles. I actually sold forty jars for five dollars each! So I kept going with it. Claudia kept working and paying all the bills. I do not know how. She is a financial budgeting wizard because she managed everything with just her income. We were no longer saving any money but we were content. We loved our home, and the city it was in, and each other. There was nothing that could break us.

I spent the first two years in the new home trying to find a job. I filled out over six hundred applications but only went on two interviews. There was nothing for me to do. Talk after talk with Claudia about things kept leaning for me to stop looking for work. She says to me, "Look Hun, don't worry about things. We got it. We don't have a daycare bill, we are eating better, living cleaner, the kids are healthier, the cars are paid off now, and I'm due for my third raise in three years. We are fine. Relax. Be OK with being at home." I really had no choice because there was no work to be found. So I embraced the role as the "stay at home dad", but not without a fight! There's just something about hearing a guy say "You let your wife be the bread winner?" It's a shot in the man card. It's a stab at the ego. A man's legend is at stake if this happens, right? Again I was wrong.

Chapter 13

SAHDlife

The acceptance to my new role was the toughest obstacle I've ever dealt with in the free world. Everything my dad taught me about being a "man" couldn't be used. Wait. Yes it can! And it was! I woke everyday as if I was going to work. My job was managing the house for our family. Since I couldn't make any money, I would save it for us. The goal for me now was to prove the old saying; a penny saved is a penny earned, was true. I was already saving us more than ten thousand dollars a year for daycare charges. I made lists each day of things to do. I would create things to do if I ran out of things to do. I made sure Claudia was ready for her trip to work every day. Our driveway is about 75 feet long uphill. I go outside every morning at 5:30am and turn her car around so she doesn't have to back it out. If it's cold out, I heat the car up, if it's hot out, I get the a/c running. In the spring, I will clip a rose from one the bushes we have around the house and place it in or on the car somewhere for her. I get her coffee ready as she walks out the door. I walk her to the car. I do everything possible to make sure she never has to stop to put fuel in it. At 5:30am when the temperature is twenty-two degrees, I take it to the gas station to fill it up so she won't have to.

I created an open end list of what I call "sah-duties". And they don't stop with my wife. I do everything I can for the kids as well. Just like a seasoned stay at home mother, nothing gets missed. Every doctor, dentist, orthodontist, psychologist, allergist, and even the veterinarian appointments are made by me and they are met on time. Not to mention the after school activities like Basketball, Soccer, and Tae Kwon Do classes. I've coached for the kid's teams, I mentor them. And of course I yell and scream a lot, but I give them what my folks could never give my sisters and me. I give them guidance and more importantly, my time.

The most unexpected positive from being a parent is I had full control of what the kids were exposed to. No violent movies or video games were allowed. I got to know everything about their friend's parents before the kids were allowed to become friends with anyone. I worked with my daughter everyday on her alphabets and numbers. I taught her how to add and subtract. At times, "Wow." I thought, "Was this really happening? I was cooking like I never had and getting better and better. I wound up creating a cooking club on Facebook because everyone I friended got such a kick out of seeing all the cooking posts between my mother and I. My garden expanded to the point of having every vegetable the family could stomach stored in the freezer, hence saving us more money! Since I was doing a hundred percent of the cooking and cleaning. I created a spread sheet of every product we buy for the weekly shopping. I have it set up like the cycle counts I used to for inventory control at the warehouses I managed. I have the price of everything, from all the major local grocery stores, even things we never buy, just because I want to be that thorough. I switched about sixty-five percent of the name brand items we use to store brands. The kids never knew the difference. I also added three trips year to buy all our paper goods, batteries and cleaning supplies from a leading wholesale store. In the end I saved us more than $700.00 a year in produce by gardening and shaved more than $2,000.00 a year with my spread sheet shopping system. And the pickles I made, took off like mad! From forty jars sold in the first year to seven hundred four jars in my fifth year! That's another $3,500.00. Not too shabby.

I loved every aspect of what I was doing. I couldn't believe I was enjoying myself being an at home dad!

I had to do some things the old fashioned way to keep it kind of macho. I cut the grass with a push mower. The yard is 27,000 square feet of some pretty tough terrain. My yard is full of big trees. There are many hills and valleys to overcome. I rake the leaves by hand. There is so much raking that needs to be done that I don't stop until I've reached four blisters! I let them heal, and then go again! We have a fireplace that Claudia absolutely loves to use so instead of paying to have wood delivered; I cut down a tree or two and use them. I do it Paul Bunyan style, by hand with an axe. I cut the trees down, then cut them up with a chainsaw but then split the logs with the axe. This saves us more money! The more things I do like this, I feel, keeps my man card active. Humorously I keep telling myself it's the only way to keep it. As I balance myself at the top of a twenty-four foot extension ladder to clean the gutters I say, "How many stay at home moms do you see doing this stuff?" I was doing so many things it was insane. Everyday my wife would come home and ask me, "So what did you do today?" She would worry because I did everything alone. So I started videotaping myself. I recorded myself doing the chores around the house like dusting, mopping and even cooking. I taped everything I did outside too, so when she asked what I did that day I would just show her the video! I showed her that I took all precautions necessary with each duty. Of course I played into the camera at times. I'd lip sync the songs that were playing on the radio at the time and say funny lines if I tripped or did something quirky. Well doing this sparked a new hobby for me. I was now making little home videos and dubbing my some of my old band's music and a few popular top forty tunes over them. I started another Facebook page called SAHDlife and posted them there. In doing all the video editing and song dubbing, I found a story in the making. I was listening to all the lyrics the band wrote and they seemed to coincide. My creative side was ignited again. I started writing a story we had already written. This one would be easy because it was here in these songs.

Then of course, in typical "why me" form, an incident would slow my role. As I was transforming the shed in the back into my mancave, an electrical fire burned it to the ground. I lost everything. All the digital and taped recordings from my twenty or so years with the band were gone. All my tools and memorabilia were incinerated. Everything I'd just written was ashes. Oh yes, Memories from when the guards burned my stuff in prison clouded my thoughts. The greenhouse was gone. When the fire broke out Claudia and I were frantic getting the kids out of the house. The shed is not attached to the house but the electricity was. While the shed burned, Claudia had the fire dept. on the phone, the kids dressed as fast as they could to get outside. The town at the time was frozen. The night before the fire we got hit with a major ice storm. Although a lot of the city was out of power, we still had ours. It was only about nine or ten degrees outside when the shed went up in flames. I watched my family run out of the front door as I finished getting myself bundled up. As I caught up to them and we found a safe place to stand, the fire department showed up. I did however have enough mental faculties to grab my camera and got some the fire recorded. I will definitely be using that footage in a video somewhere! Everybody was safe, no one got hurt. Emotionally I was devastated. The loss was great to me because everything I had to show my efforts through life were gone. They may have been failures but they were proof I gave it my all. What do I do? Take the pain.

The insurance money was enough to replace the shed but I figured to save some of it by rebuilding it myself. I had enough knowledge in carpentry to handle it. I would build it bigger and better and I could design it as an actual mancave to my specifications. In addition to the money saved, it would be so much more personal, with it being from the sweat of my brow. And so I did! It turned out to be a bit more than I could chew but after everything I've been through in my life this was no problem. I just took things one at a time. I got frustrated a few times and my kids saw it. I thought about what they would think if I gave up. I couldn't let that happen. I didn't want to give up. I gave up on my goals because of other people involved. I didn't want my kids to see me give up on myself. It's kind of like this book. The kids know I'm writing it. I tell them sure I hope it sells and makes money. But that's not the goal. I just want to finish it. Just like the man cave, I just want to finish it. I told them it doesn't matter if this book fails. It's ok. My goal was to finish it. It's a natural instinct to keep trying. I guess haven't really given up on reaching my goals now have I? In my heart I still want to achieve that status of "rich & famous" but it's just not that important to me anymore. Just having the kids witnessing me finish what I start will be enough.

Wouldn't it be ironic if someone was to take this story to Hollywood? What if it happens like with my first script and they just want my story, not me. You better believe I would jump all over it. I guess if you ever see the movie you know that happened.

Claudia and I woke one day at our usual 5am time. She shut off the alarm and began stretching. I laid there smiling in the dark at her silhouette. She's so beautiful. As I savored the moment, the next thought was I had to be outside in freezing temperatures in a few minutes to heat her car up. I didn't have to but I always want to. I had a hundred other sahduties on my list for the day. I didn't mind. I really do enjoy what I do. I hopped up as my wife turned on the bathroom light and shut the door. I made the bed, got dressed, grabbed her stuff and headed outside. I often shut the door and think of Henry Hill at this point. Do you know the last scene from the movie "Good Fellas" where Henry (Ray

Liotta) steps out of his house to get the daily newspaper from the steps? He's in the federal witness program and looks in the camera as he's narrating the final line. He says, "Today everything is different. There's no action. I have to wait around like everyone else. You can't even get descent food. Right after I got here I ordered spaghetti with marinara sauce and I got egg noodles and ketchup. I'm an average nobody. I get to live the rest of my life like a schnook."

I'm good with it. I'm happy. I love how things turned out. I know it won't be like this forever but at this time, at 5:30 am while I turned Claudia's car around in the driveway and got the heater cranking. I stopped on the bottom step and looked up at the house. I was smiling. This was it. This was happiness.

Chapter 14

Validation

I've heard that saying, "Everything happen for a reason." countless times and from me to you. I don't believe it. I think things just happen and how you respond is the outcome. I believe what we gain in knowledge from good and a bad situation is up to us, but a reason for something happening? Nahhh. I don't buy it. We strengthen or weaken from things. What happens next is our move, But not for any reason. It just is what it is. Take my sister Linda for instance; she was wacked out of her mind on crack. She lost her kids and her life three times from it. What's the reason for that? I mean we know what caused it, but there was no reason. Her reactions are what matter. After my father was awarded custody of her children from the state, she woke up. Perhaps the brushes with death did it, but she found a way to kick the habit. It wasn't through any rehab program or a jail sentence. She did it on her own and basically cold turkey. She cleaned herself up and started working. Headstrong and driven she beat the addiction. She spent ten years paying child support and cleared her name with the state. She is a functioning member of society and a tax payer. She even met a man and fell in love and is now married! And as her children became of legal age under my dad's care, they all went back to her. They were making up for lost time I suppose, but also to share the only thing that truly makes us happy as human beings, family time. I am proud of Linda. She did something that hardly anyone in her position is able to do. But to say there is reason for her to go through what she went through is absurd.

Was there any reason for anything I endured? Was I supposed to grow through life the way I did so that I could be the person I am today? No. I am who I am because of what I went through. Is there some mysterious being watching me just to see what I do when something bad happens? I don't think so.

There are going to be a number of people who read this and I'm sure emotions will flare. I said a lot of things here that will strike a nerve or two. I'm sorry. But I did it for a reason. (LOL!)

There will be people who'll read this and call "bullshit" on it. They'll say whatever comes to mind and argue the tales. They have the right to their own opinions. Everything I've written will be ripped apart by those people who love to rip things apart. Then again, there will be people who like it and will say good things. I just have to take the good with the bad.

I've had my share of people calling me a liar. In school I would share stories of my adventures and there were a few that never believed me. No prisoner I spent time with ever believed a word I said.

But one time, a man stuck up for me. He understood a guy like me. He understood speaking. He knew that when someone was speaking, another was listening. So if you have something to say, say it in a way that will keep the attention of those listening. This very intelligent man was the host of a call-in radio talk show. Dr. Dick Richardson. The show was The Dove Loctors. I called often. So often that Dr. Dick and the other host Dr. Something, and other regular callers knew my voice. I knew theirs too!

My last call to them was probably my greatest call! The topic was the strangest things people have done. So I call in with a tale about me and the neighbor lady Cindy from my childhood. She had me one time place my foot in her vagina and wiggle my toes. I chose the correct words to deliver the story very carefully so they wouldn't dump me off the air. The story is quite shocking but when delivered correctly, it's very funny. The hosts were all laughing hysterically. I got my laugh and that was my cue to let the next caller on. The next few calls were responses to my story. The last one said, "Hey guys, you can't believe that guy. He's so full of it!" Dr. Dick belts back with dominating conviction, "Hey! Do you understand what it is we do here? We're just killing time and selling commercials. It's a radio talk show. I don't care if it's the truth. I don't care if everything he says is conjured up in his sick little mind. It doesn't matter to me, as long as what he says and the stories he tells, are absolutely spectacular! I will let him on the air every time he calls!" Thanks Dr. Dick. You get it. I'm not saying anything, I'm just saying...

Chapter 15

Gone from here

My parents died about eighteen months apart while I was in my mid-forties. Both had visited me and my family at the home Claudia and I purchased to raise the kids. My mother was happy with how I turned out. She saw me doing all the house work and cooking and how good I was with the kids. She actually had a problem with how strict I was with them! Ha! If that didn't beat all! (Pun intended) but she was proud of her boy. She'd never envisioned me in the situation I was living. She wouldn't have believed it if she didn't witness it. Yes she would, who am I kidding? She is the one who trained me! Ironically she was secretly pissed off at me and never told me because two years after she died I found out she had left some money for all my sisters but not me. She left what was supposed to be mine to my nephew.

My father, he became my best friend. I had, for the last ten years of his life, the guy I saw having fun and joking around with his friends, at my side, joking around with me.

And I cherish every moment. My favorite moment is the day he said he was proud of me.

I'm a failure. It's a fact. I'm proud to say it. I'm a failure. It means I tried. I did everything I needed to do to succeed but always came up short. I almost made it a couple times, but almost don't count.

In my last conversation with my father I told him I was ok with being a failure. Success was important to me but I learned it's not the most important thing. Family is. He said, "Well what do you know? My boy grew up, failed at everything, and won in

The End"

Printed in the United States
By Bookmasters